P9-DFY-279

CINNAMON MOON

CINNAMON MOON

TESS HILMO

MARGARET FERGUSON BOOKS
Farrar Straus Giroux
New York

Farrar Straus Giroux Books for Young Readers
An imprint of Macmillan Publishing Group, LLC
175 Fifth Avenue, New York 10010

Printed in the United States of America by LSC Communications US, LLC (Lakeside Classic),
Harrisonburg, Virginia
Designed by Roberta Pressel
First edition, 2016
10 9 8 7 6 5 4 3 2 1

mackids.com

Library of Congress Cataloging-in-Publication Data

Names: Hilmo, Tess, author.
Title: Cinnamon moon / Tess Hilmo.
Description: First edition. | New York : Margaret Ferguson Books/Farrar Straus Giroux,
    2016. | Summary: "Historical fiction about two siblings and a friend trying to
    find a new family and a home after the Great Chicago Fire"—Provided by
    publisher.
Identifiers: LCCN 2015036345 | ISBN 9780374302825 (hardback) |
    ISBN 9780374302832 (e-book)
Subjects: | CYAC: Great Fire, Chicago, Ill., 1871—Fiction. | Refugees—Fiction. |
    Brothers and sisters—Fiction. | BISAC: JUVENILE FICTION / Historical /
    United States / 19th Century. | JUVENILE FICTION / Family / Siblings.
Classification: LCC PZ7.H566 Ci 2016 | DDC [Fic]3—dc23
LC record available at http://lccn.loc.gov/2015036345

Our books may be purchased in bulk for promotional, educational, or business use. Please
contact your local bookseller or the Macmillan Corporate and Premium Sales Department
at (800) 221-7945 ext. 5442 or by e-mail at MacmillanSpecialMarkets@macmillan.com.

For Gertrude and Ida.
And for my mother, Sarah.

CHICAGO
SATURDAY, NOVEMBER 25, 1871

A long, delicate twist of ash still lingers in the sky above the Irish quarter of Chicago. It is two blocks over from where I stand on the porch of the boardinghouse where my younger brother, Quinn, and I have been living for the past seven weeks. The sky here is steel gray, but clear. A cold November wind glides and flutters above the rooftops. The same wind that drove Chicago's Great Fire last month has since been slowly, gently scrubbing it out of the sky.

I look at the ash cloud and wonder if the darkest, middle spot is lingering over the O'Learys' barn. Everyone is blaming Mrs. O'Leary and one of her cows for starting the fire that destroyed most of Chicago.

"You've done your best to help them," Quinn says, coming

up to my side. He knows my thoughts by the direction of my gaze.

"A pound of bacon isn't much."

"Plus the flour and eggs from before . . ."

"I feel so bad for them," I say. "Nobody really knows how that fire started."

"Ailis," Quinn asks, "why do you risk taking things from Miss Franny's kitchen?"

Miss Franny runs this boardinghouse. Father would have called her a skinflint or pinchpenny—which just means greedy. I'd add spiteful, prejudiced, and mean to the list.

"Mrs. O'Leary has lost her milking business and hardly comes outside anymore," I say to Quinn. "Giving her and her family food is a small thing, but maybe it lets them know someone cares."

"You know stealing food from the kitchen only makes Miss Franny angry at them—and at you."

"Miss Franny is eternally angry at me, and at you, and at the O'Learys, because we're Irish. It doesn't matter what we do."

"She'll make you go without dinner tonight and you'll probably get a whipping."

I look over to my brother, whose dark eyes are heavy with worry. The way they crowd his nose reminds me of Father. "Quinn the protector," I say, tousling his hair. "Don't worry so much about me."

He dips his gaze down and says, "You're all I have." The truth of his words makes the air between us uncomfortable.

"It's precisely for that reason you must trust me," I say. "You're only eleven."

"And you're only twelve," he says. Then he reaches into his back pocket and pulls out a newspaper. "Look what I have. Today's *Chicago Tribune*."

"Where'd you get it?" I ask, grabbing the paper and sitting down on the front step. It's chilly outside, but we are away from Miss Franny's watchful gaze.

"I found it in the kitchen."

I start to flip through the pages of the *Tribune*. The whole neighborhood has been buzzing about Mr. and Mrs. O'Leary being called before the city's investigative council and I want to read about it. But first I want to see if there is any mention of the fire that happened in our hometown of Peshtigo, Wisconsin.

"Ailis—" Quinn begins.

"Don't start up again," I say, looking at Quinn.

"But Miss Franny has let us stay out of kindness when we have nowhere else to go. Maybe you can at least *try* to annoy her less."

"Not out of kindness," I correct. "Out of obligation to Mr. Olsen. Don't forget that he's the one who owns this boardinghouse. Miss Franny is just an employee."

Mr. Olsen is a real estate investor and former president of the great Union Pacific Railroad Company. He has been trying to build a railroad line from Chicago up to Peshtigo. Father was an important liaison between the Peshtigo farmers and the railroad executives. I know Mr. Olsen wanted to buy our land for the railroad, but Father wouldn't sell it. Still, Father arranged meetings and encouraged others to at least listen to the railroad company's plan. I guess Mr. Olsen sees helping Quinn and me as a way to pay back some of Father's kindness. I tell myself he has no idea of the type of person Miss Franny truly is and that he would not have placed us in her care otherwise.

Quinn settles down on the step next to me and leans in to my side, trying to get a glimpse of the newspaper. He can't read nearly as well as I can because Father needed him in the cranberry bogs most of the year. Farming and schooling are often at odds. "Is it there?" he asks.

I look through all the pages. "Nothing."

Quinn shakes his head. "How can that be? I overheard Sam say the count of dead bodies is over two thousand for Peshtigo's fire—that is nearly ten times as deadly as Chicago's fire. And it happened on the same day! How can there not even be a mention of it in the paper?"

Sam is one of Miss Franny's boarders and the only one I pay any attention to, mostly because he is the only one who bothers to speak to Quinn and me. That, and the fact he doesn't switch out like the others. He has been at Miss Franny's since before we came. It was Quinn who first noticed that Miss Franny cuts a thicker slice of roast for Sam and fills his coffee cup before it is even empty.

"Peshtigo is not Chicago. A poor lumber-and-farming town doesn't have the world looking at it. It's the big city that gets the press. Besides, you shouldn't be earwigging on Sam's conversations."

"And you shouldn't be stealing Miss Franny's bacon."

"One-tenth of which was mine already."

Just as the ring of my words leaves the air, Miss Franny steps out onto the porch.

Willow switch in hand, she narrows her eyes at the sight of me.

• • •

I am curled up in the bed I share with Nettie when she slides in beside me. My face is to the wall and her cold feet bump against my legs, sending a shiver through my body. The bed is in the storage closet off the back of the house because Nettie always has a runny nose. Other tenants complained so Miss Franny keeps her separated on account of their fear of getting sick. At least there is a small window.

Nettie is only six years old and had lived her whole life in one of Chicago's orphanages until it burned down. City leaders asked anyone who had space to take in those displaced by the fire and promised a small monthly payment for doing so. The children in the orphanage were handed off to various locations, and that's how Nettie came to Miss Franny's.

When Mr. Olsen delivered Quinn and me to the boardinghouse after the weeklong trip from Peshtigo, Miss Franny asked the guests who would be willing to share their space. I'll never forget standing there at Mr. Olsen's side when Nettie's sweet hand went into the air, offering her bed.

Quinn ended up on the front room floor.

"Are you awake, Ailis?" Nettie whispers in the dark.

"Yes."

"I'm sorry about Miss Franny. I don't think she wants to be mean. Not really."

Precious Nettie, who shares her tiny bed and forgives people like Miss Franny.

"She's just so . . ."—her words trail off—"tired."

I want to remind Nettie that Miss Franny seemed plenty awake when she was bellowing at Quinn about the woodpile or giving me three lashes with a willow switch for swiping the bacon, but it seems pointless.

"I brought you something."

I turn from the wall. "Oh, Nettie, you should never take anything from the kitchen."

She giggles. "It's not food. It's the newspaper. Quinn said you'd want it back."

"How did you get it away from Miss Franny?"

"I hid it in the waistband of my bloomers when she wasn't looking. Do you still want to read it after it was in my bloomers?"

"Shhh," I say, reminding us both to lower our voices. "Of course I do." Suddenly the night doesn't seem so miserable.

She hands me the paper and I put it under my pillow. "Better not light the lamp when Miss Franny is in such a bad mood," I say. "We'll read it in the morning, together."

"But I'm not tired," Nettie says.

"Close your eyes, sleep will come."

"No it won't. Ailis, tell me a story."

I punch at my pillow. "What kind of story?"

"A story about home."

Nettie always wants to hear about families and homes because it's something she's never had.

"How about a mermaid story instead? Or a story about a magical nymph from Ireland?"

"No," she says. "Just a story about how your mother would do things."

I don't want to think about how Mother did things.

Still, it's Nettie.

"Okay," I say. "Mother had long hair the color of clouds at sunset."

"Reddish orange, just like yours."

I remember Mother's long braids twisted up on her head. They were so beautiful. "Everyone loved her hair, especially Father."

"Father was a cranberry farmer," Nettie says. She talks about them as if they were her own.

"Yes. He worked long days and was tired at night, but always managed to play the fiddle before bedtime."

"He was a wonderful musician. His fiddle is right there in the corner." She motions in the darkness toward the foot of the bed where Quinn and I keep our things, including the badly charred case that holds Father's fiddle. How it survived the fire, I'll never know.

"That's right," I say. "And he was good with stories, too. He liked to tell this one about mischievous fairies who hide behind a looking glass and . . ."

"No," Nettie says softly. "No fairy stories tonight. Just family stories."

"All right." I take a breath and settle my memory into the farmhouse back in Peshtigo. I am grateful for the cover of darkness in Nettie's closet because I can allow the tears to come as I remember Father holding his fiddle in his calloused hands, bending and swaying as he played "Johnny, I Hardly Knew Ye." "Mother would pull Gertrude up on her lap by the fireplace . . ."

"Gertrude was three, right, Ailis?"

"Yes," I say, remembering Gertrude's chubby pink cheeks. "She was only three."

"I would have loved Gertrude, wouldn't I have, Ailis?"

"And she would have loved you right back."

"What kind of games did Gertrude like to play?"

I can't help but smile. "Hide-and-seek was her favorite. She'd hide in the wool basket almost every time."

"But you and Quinn would pretend you didn't know where she was, right?"

"Yes."

"You'd say, *Oh my, where could Gertrude be hiding?*"

I turn to the side and wipe my wet cheek along the pillow edge.

"Where would I have hidden, Ailis?" Nettie asks.

"I don't know. Maybe in the wool basket as well," I suggest.

"No," she says. "I would never take Gertrude's spot. I think I'd hide under the table. Did Mother keep a cloth over the table? If she did, I could hide there."

"For you, I'm sure she would have."

"She was such a good mother, wasn't she, Ailis?"

I try to say yes, but all that comes out is a squeak. Nettie takes my hand under the quilt.

"Thanks for that story," she says. "I know it makes you sad, but you had something real special. Maybe just for twelve years, but at least you had it."

And all I can think as I listen to Nettie's breath slow as she falls asleep is, *Twelve years is not enough.*

2

Nettie is up and off to church when I awake. It is Sunday morning and I can hear hammers slamming against nails and stone. The great rebuilding of Chicago is constant, even on weekends. It's all under official order from Chicago's brand-new mayor, Joseph Medill.

Sam tells me he sees Mayor Medill downtown from time to time, standing on stages and waving banners, talking about how Chicago's loss is the greatest in all history. He brags about how he has reached out to a bunch of powerful world leaders, who are sending fat checks to help with the rebuilding. He says the money will make Chicago stronger than ever before.

Peshtigo did get a train car full of blankets and clothes

right after the fire, but there will be no fat checks coming in from overseas. No one is waving banners at our loss.

One evening, as I was washing the dishes, I mentioned these thoughts to Quinn, and Miss Franny overheard. She said I was a wicked child for questioning Chicago's misfortune and maybe she's right. If I think about it long enough, I know Miss Franny has a fair point when she says Chicago's loss was also a terrible thing.

But knowing my feelings are wrong doesn't change them. So I keep them to myself.

"Ailis Doyle, you lazy girl, get up this instant," Miss Franny hollers from the kitchen.

"Yes, Miss Franny," I holler back, putting on my skirt and blouse. I recover the *Tribune* from under my pillow and follow Nettie's lead of sliding it into the front of my bloomers, under my blouse and held in place by my skirt's waistband. Then I twist my hair into a braid, looking out the tiny window into the side yard where Sam and Quinn are busy removing weathered slats from the side of an old shed. Sam is prying the rotten boards off with a crowbar and Quinn is stacking them up by the woodpile.

"You'd sleep the day away if I didn't get after you," Miss Franny says, coming into the small room. She is a conundrum. Tall and slender. Younger than she should be as mistress of a boardinghouse. Pretty, some might even say.

That is until she opens her mouth.

Quinn says it's her mouth that keeps her unmarried and I've no reason to disagree.

Miss Franny begins waving a small trowel in my face. "Get the potatoes," she says. "I need a full basket."

"Yes, ma'am."

"Fill the holes behind you."

"Yes, ma'am."

"And don't track mud into my kitchen when you come back. This isn't wretched Peshtigo. Take your shoes off at the door."

I dip my chin but don't reply with a *yes, ma'am*. Peshtigo is not wretched. It is towering timbers and brilliant blue skies. It is still-water lakes and green pastures.

Miss Franny notices my silence and smacks the trowel on the side of my arm. She is a miserable woman.

"I'll remove my shoes," is all I can bring myself to say.

She drops the trowel at my feet and returns to the kitchen. "Stupid rat," she mutters.

I pick up the trowel and think about my schoolmaster back home. Mr. Frankel was from Germany. He couldn't teach us much about spelling or conjugation, but he knew more about animals than anyone I had ever met. Father said he was a biologist in Munich but gave it all up to bring his family to America. Even if that meant spending his days in

15

a ramshackle schoolhouse. If Mr. Frankel were here, he would inform Miss Franny that rats are surprisingly intelligent. But Mr. Frankel is gone with the rest of them so I say nothing and go outside.

The community garden is a chunk of land owned by the city and farmed by anyone in the neighborhood who wants to participate. Everyone plants what they can and shares what comes out. It is meant to supplement people's own gardens and also allow those who live as boarders to have an opportunity to farm a little. Sam says in the summer there are glorious things like tomatoes and basil and hot peppers. But now that it's November, just potatoes remain.

Next to the garden is a row of walnut trees, tall and majestic. Our neighbor, Mrs. Mead, is the only one digging potatoes, probably because it is Sunday and most people are at their various churches. Miss Franny never asks Quinn and me if we want to attend church, not that I would go anyway. Mother and Father dragged the whole family to Catholic Mass every single week, but what good did it do us when the wind turned to fire?

"Mornin', Ailis," Mrs. Mead calls out with a raised hand.

I grin and wave and then scoot around one of the walnut trees. I cannot wait another minute to look at the newspaper.

I reach inside my coat, under my blouse, and pull it out.

"Found you!"

I jump with fright, but it is only Nettie sneaking up from behind.

"You promised you'd share it," she says, pointing to the paper. "And now you're running off to read it without me."

I show her the trowel. "I'm getting the potatoes. You're the one who left so early."

"I went to say my prayers and light a candle." Nettie pushes into my side. "You should come to church with me. Father Farlane is awful nice."

"Who would I light a candle for?" I ask, flipping through the paper.

"For Quinn." Her eyes are wide with a sort of hope. "Or me."

"I wish lighting a candle would fix things, Nettie, but it won't." I keep turning the pages of the newspaper until I come to page 6. "Here it is! *The Great Fire*," I read. *"Mrs. O'Leary, the owner of the cow, etc., examined."*

"What does it say?"

"It's just a short one-paragraph summary," I answer. "I'm not even sure it can be trusted." Both the *Chicago Evening Journal* and the *Chicago Tribune* have been printing false stories since the fire. The *Journal* seems to be the worst, reporting outright lies about the O'Leary family. One article said Catherine O'Leary was a dirty hag, over seventy years old, who bragged about starting the fire to get back at the city because she was cut off from financial aid, but anyone who knows the family knows that isn't true. I'd guess Catherine O'Leary to be in her early forties and up until the fire, her business was successful, so she had no need to ask for a free dime from anyone.

Of course, the residents of Chicago don't bother to verify the newspaper stories. They are desperate for answers—and an old Irish hag is the perfect person to blame.

Even if that person doesn't exist.

"Read it out loud," Nettie pleads. "Don't skip a word."

I read about how Mrs. O'Leary said she and her family went to bed and were awakened by their neighbor, Daniel Sullivan, who told them their barn was on fire. Mrs. O'Leary also testified that the McLaughlin family, who lived in the front part of their house, were having a small party that night and had possibly gone to the barn to get some milk. "That's all it says."

Nettie slumps back against the tree. "Who do you think started the fire, Ailis?"

"Hard to say. Mr. Sullivan saw it first, which is making some wonder about him."

"I know Mr. Sullivan," Nettie says, perking up. "He's only got one leg. The other one is made out of wood." She reaches down and knocks her hand on her lower leg. "He's too nice to do something like that."

"That's what I think, too," I say. "And there's also been talk about some boys gambling in the barn that night. Then there's the McLaughlins' party that should be considered."

"Ailis"—Nettie's voice is soft—"do you know what started your fire?"

I fold the newspaper, remembering the winds of that afternoon and how they suddenly turned to flame. How Quinn and I were coming home from the general store when we saw a wide and twisting wall of fire spinning across the land. How I pulled him into the Menominee River and forced his head down under the water over and over so we wouldn't burn. Then walking back across town two hours later, stepping over charred lumps of animals and heaven knows what else—only to find a black square where our farmhouse used to be. We recognized Mother and Father by part of Father's boot that was oddly unburned and Gertrude in Mother's arms.

I tighten my grip on the paper and push all those thoughts away. "No," I say to Nettie's question. "Does it matter? Would it make any difference if I knew that a couple of the lumberjacks got in a drunken fight and knocked over a lamp? Or that some kid across town was playing with fire in a field?"

Nettie's chin tips down, quivering.

"This is my whole point with the O'Learys," I go on.

"The damage is done. No one did it on purpose. Why ruin more lives?"

Nettie bobs her head twice.

"Come on," I say, standing up and reaching a hand out. "Help me dig up these potatoes before it gets any later and Miss Franny has a conniption fit."

3

Nettie helps me search the community garden. I use the trowel to dig in the frozen dirt, which is challenging. We only find three potatoes—two of which are mealy and discolored on the side—and throw them in the basket. After searching with the trowel we go back through every row, feeling for sprouts or lumps with our hands. Finally, we give up. I take the basket and we start walking to Miss Franny's.

"People have lost their homes and jobs because of the fire," I say. "They're hungry. Besides, the potatoes can't last forever. It's not our fault they're gone."

"Mrs. Mead got the last of them," Nettie says in her gentle way. "If we weren't reading the paper, we could have asked her to share before she left." Then she looks off to the side. "They're probably already cut up into a pot. Should we go ask her to share them?"

"The Meads volunteered to take in two families," I say. "So much of Chicago was lost, people are doubling up on living quarters. The Meads need those potatoes more than we do." I put my arm around Nettie's shoulder and pull her in. "We will be fine."

"We will?"

"Positively, absolutely, perfectly fine," I promise.

"Miss Franny won't be happy when she sees these three ugly potatoes."

"They are sad-looking things," I say.

Nettie points to the smallest. "That one's all shriveled up like my toes when I've been in the bathwater too long."

It feels good to see the hint of a smile behind her eyes. "This one's fatter, but has spots on it," I say, pointing to the largest potato. "It looks like Miss Franny's face before she puts on all that powder."

Nettie covers her mouth and giggles.

"Look, there's Charlie!" Nettie says, heading across the street.

"Watch for buggies," I yell, going after her.

She stops on the other side of the street in front of a broad-shouldered man in a plaid flannel shirt. His head is as bald as an eagle's, but he has black, curly hair pouring out of the front of his shirt collar and spinning in knots on the backs of his hands.

"Charlie is our cook at the orphanage," Nettie says. "He's the best cook in the whole world. Are you still making your rabbit stew, Charlie?"

"Not so much these days," he says. A toothpick dangles from the corner of his mouth, bouncing as he speaks.

"Too bad," Nettie says.

Charlie sits down on his heels so he can look at Nettie straight on. I notice his shoes are shiny blue-black leather with a silver buckle on the front. "Don't worry about me, Net," he says. "I'll be back cooking for my favorite boys and girls soon. They've already started rebuilding the orphanage. Where are you staying now? And who is your friend here?"

"This is Ailis. She's almost my sister and we're staying at Miss Franny's boardinghouse in the prettiest room you ever did see and Miss Franny gives us chores just like a real mom would and even cooks us dinner but it's not as good as your stew."

"Did you say that all in one breath?" Charlie asks with a smile. Then he pulls on one of her braids gently and says, "Same old Nettie."

Nettie throws her arms around him. "I miss you, Charlie."

He seems surprised by her gesture and gives her a quick pat on the back. Then he stands up and repositions his toothpick to the other side of his mouth. "I'll see you around, kid."

"You should come visit me," Nettie says, waving as we walk away.

Charlie keeps to his spot on the road, watching us for a minute before turning back in the opposite direction.

"Don't tell strangers where you're staying," I say.

"Charlie's not a stranger. I've known him my whole life. Besides, what if he came to Miss Franny's and cooked his stew for us? You'd like his stew. It's good."

I guide Nettie across the street and say, "Race you to the boardinghouse?"

"On your mark," Nettie says. "Get set . . ." And then she takes off running and yells, "Go!" after she is a good distance ahead.

I hold back, allowing her to keep her lead and taking in the world around me. Gauzy clouds cloak the sky and cover up the sun, making everything colorless and drab. People shuffle by, wrapped in dark woolen coats or shawls. I notice their freezing white breath puffing out as they go. They are human locomotives pushing through the city.

And everywhere, from all directions, there is still the sound of hammers and chisels and workmen shouting commands at one another.

"You didn't even try," Nettie says as I jog up the walk of the boardinghouse.

"Tried my best," I lie. "But it was clear you would win so it seemed silly to keep running full speed."

She eyes me suspiciously and then turns her attention to the basket. "I'm afraid to take these inside."

"You go in the front and I'll take these around back to the kitchen," I say. "You weren't assigned potatoes so you don't have to worry about what Miss Franny thinks. Let me handle her."

Nettie runs her hand back and forth under her nose. It is what she does when she feels uneasy.

"Go on," I say.

"It's just that . . ." Her hand keeps going under her nose—side to side.

"Quit hovering and go find Quinn."

Nettie stops rubbing her nose and gives a tiny nod. "Okay, Ailis," she says.

I watch her go through the front door and then I walk around back, remembering to take my shoes off outside the kitchen door. The mud on the streets is too frozen to be messy, so they are mostly clean, but I take them off all the same.

A push of warm air and the smell of logs burning in the stove meet me as I come into the kitchen. For a moment, it seems welcoming. Friendly, even. I place the basket on the table and start for the hallway but Miss Franny steps into the doorway, blocking my path.

"Where do you think you're going?" she asks, swishing her skirt as she moves forward.

"To my room," I say.

"And if you go to your room, who will peel the potatoes for supper?"

Every inch of my being wants to say, *you*. Instead, I turn to the basket and pull out the potatoes. "I will prepare them for dinner, Miss Franny."

My back is turned, so I don't see the look on her face when she realizes the basket only holds one good potato and two shrunken ones, but I hear her gasp and feel a ripple of anger roll through the room.

"Where are our potatoes?" she asks. I had expected her to yell as she so often does, but her voice is steady and firm. "You gave them to the O'Learys, didn't you?" She takes the empty basket and shoves it into my chest. "Well, you can get back out there and dig some more for me."

"There are no more potatoes. The garden is empty."

Miss Franny slits her eyes and leans in. Her breath brushes across my face. "You gave the last of the potatoes to that filthy family?"

"I didn't give them anything," I say. "The garden was empty when I got there. I checked every row but only found these three."

She keeps pressing her lips together and staring at me

26

through a seething squint. "You gave our potatoes to that filthy family and now you stand here in my kitchen and lie about it."

Something about the depth of her anger makes me feel unsteady. "I didn't, I swear it, Miss Franny. I didn't give them anything."

"You did and we both know it. Look at you, filthy just like them."

I glance down and notice my dress is black with dirt. "It's because I was on my hands and knees," I say. "It's because I was digging through every inch of the field trying to make you happy."

"A filthy liar, standing in my kitchen and sweating like a pig."

A sharpness snaps deep inside of me and, in a flash, fear turns into frustration. "Shows what you know," I say, straightening my spine. "Pigs don't even sweat."

I feel her hand hit my face before I see it, she is so fast. There is still a ringing in my ears when she says, "Get the red hen."

"What?"

"I have eight other people expecting Sunday supper later today and you've brought me nothing. Go get the red hen."

"Why not one of the gray hens?"

"Because I say so. That sickly girl keeps feeding our scraps to the red one. It's the fattest."

She's talking about Nettie's favorite hen, the one Nettie named Kristina. I think it's foolish to name something that will eventually end up stewed with turnips. Still, I know Nettie doesn't understand that. Six is so young. Kristina is fatter than the other hens, but that isn't why Miss Franny wants to put her in a stew. She is doing it to punish me because she knows I love Nettie and Nettie loves Kristina.

"Fine," I say.

"And while you are getting the hen, I will call the girl to help pull its feathers."

I let the door slam loudly behind me. I put on my shoes and go out to the side yard where Kristina is digging her claws through the frozen earth, looking for seeds and clueless about the plan Miss Franny has for her. But in that moment, I also have a plan.

I scoop Kristina into my arms and take off running toward the Irish quarter. Kristina is wriggling, twisting, and pecking me like mad. Chickens are surprisingly difficult to hold. Their feathers are slick and they squirm like nobody's business. Plus, Kristina is known for her temper and has never liked me to begin with.

"I'm trying to save your life," I shout. "Stop pecking at me!"

She struggles against my grasp and twists sharply to the left, flipping out of my arms and landing on the ground. Kristina shakes her feathers and glares at me. Then she begins scratching and pecking at the road as if nothing has happened.

"Stupid bird," I say.

"She got away from you, did she?" It is Mr. Sullivan.

"Hello, Mr. Sullivan."

"Call me Pegleg, everyone does."

I'm not really comfortable calling someone by their one imperfect quality so I say, "My parents always taught me to use Mr. or Mrs. or Miss."

Mr. Sullivan rubs the gray, bristly stubble spotting his chin. "Properly raised," he says with a nod. "They must be smiling down from above."

It's not a secret Quinn and I are orphans who came to the city after the fires—or that Mr. Olsen set us up in Miss Franny's boardinghouse.

Kristina pecks at Mr. Sullivan's boot.

"She's a feisty old girl, isn't she? Shall I help you take her back home?"

"That boardinghouse is not my home."

Mr. Sullivan raises an eyebrow. "'S that so? Where would you be callin' home, then?"

His brogue is deep and melodic. The rhythm of it

reminds me of Father's voice. I keep my head down, looking at Kristina. "I'm not sure."

"I know you go by Ailis, but what is your family name?"

"Doyle."

"A more Irish name I've never heard," Mr. Sullivan says. "It's a tough situation for our people in today's Chicago. Work is hard to find, but especially for us. Most of the city is angry at the Irish, even if the fire's not really our fault. Miss Franny may be a hardheaded woman, but keep yer chin up and yer mouth closed and these times will pass. Take this old man's word for it." He reaches down and picks Kristina up. "The trick is to hold 'em firm and let 'em know who's in charge." Then he grabs her feet and flips her upside down. "Here's how you do it."

"All right," I say.

"Shall I go with you?"

"No," I say. "I'm fine."

"That's a good lassie," Mr. Sullivan says. "Don't dilly about. You aren't dressed for the weather."

"I won't."

Mr. Sullivan hands me the hen, tips his hat, and walks on.

Kristina wriggles. "Come on," I say to the flailing bird, "let's get you somewhere safe."

I walk through an alleyway and around to a house two streets over from where I began. There is a small brood of chickens behind a fence: one black, two gray, and two red. I know this house belongs to the McGintys, who sell eggs to Bennie's Drug Store. These chickens are for laying and not for eating.

I look around to be sure no one is watching, then I trade Kristina for the fattest of their red hens and go back to the boardinghouse.

I hear Nettie's cries as soon as I come through the door. She is crumpled into the corner of the kitchen with her knees pulled up to her chest and her head hanging down. Quinn is at her side, trying to console her. When he hears the door swing open, he looks up and, seeing me, says, "Miss Franny is going to kill Kristina."

"No, she's not," I whisper, holding the new hen out in front of me.

Nettie looks up. I can tell by her expression that she is confused, but also that she knows this hen is not Kristina. "I swapped her out," I say. "She's safe in the McGintys' pen and you can visit her every day if you like."

Nettie wipes her eyes and then her nose and then her eyes again with the heel of her hand. "Honest?"

"See for yourself." I thrust the hen forward.

"She's nowhere near as pretty as Kristina," Nettie says. "And she doesn't have those three white feathers on her chest."

"But here is the key: you must act upset. Miss Franny is doing this to punish me through you. If she suspects it isn't working, she may do something worse."

"There is nothing worse than killing Kristina."

"Still, you must play the part and never tell anyone what we know."

"I promise, Ailis."

Quinn shakes his head and smiles.

At that moment, Miss Franny bustles in. "Where have you been?" Then she turns to Quinn, annoyed. "This is none of your concern. Are you finished mending the shed?"

"Almost," he says.

"Almost is not yes. Get to work."

"Yes, ma'am." He gives me another smile on his way out but I hold my lips in a grim line and look down at the hen. "She escaped as soon as I opened the gate and I had to chase her down the road."

Miss Franny looks at the bird. I hold my breath. Nettie whimpers in the corner.

"Oh, quit your whining," Miss Franny says. "Your nose will start running and no one will be able to stand being around you."

"Are you certain we can't kill one of the gray hens?" I ask, playing the part.

Miss Franny pulls the hatchet down from a high shelf. "If I say it's the red one, it will be the red one."

Nettie lets out a thin moan. It is perfect.

"She who gave away the last of our potatoes will have the honor of swinging the ax," Miss Franny says, holding it out to me. The hen is flapping like mad. "Go on then. We will be watching from the window." She reaches down and pulls Nettie up by the shoulder of her dress.

I take the hen out back, to the chopping block. I hear Nettie scream when the ax falls. Once it's done, I hang the hen upside down and allow the blood to drain like Mother taught me and then take it into Miss Franny's kitchen.

"Both of you can pluck it and clean it out."

"Yes, ma'am," Nettie and I say in unison.

"And I hope it serves as a lesson to you." Miss Franny is talking to me. "When the bird is prepared, put it in a pot of water and place it on the stove. Leave the feet and innards in the bowl on the table. One hen can be made into four meals if we're prudent."

"Yes, ma'am," I say again.

She stands there another minute, almost as if she is trying to decide if the punishment was sufficient or if she should send a little more misery my way. Finally, she turns and leaves the kitchen.

"Thank you," Nettie whispers as she begins pulling out the feathers.

"You did a good job," I say. "And now we get chicken soup for dinner instead of the same old potato hash."

"I love chicken soup."

I take a knife from the drawer. "Me too."

As I slice the hen's belly open, I make a promise to myself to free us from Miss Franny's grasp. I can't stand to live with her temper and cruelty. It's as if each moment I spend inside these walls is slowly changing the person I am meant to be. As if I might never become the Ailis my parents hoped for. Even if I went to Mr. Olsen and pleaded for him to move us, where would we go? This is his only boardinghouse. And besides, what would happen to Nettie? I pull the innards from the hen, drop them into the bowl, and vow to find a solution. Somehow, we will get out.

4

Monday morning, I am awakened by the usual sounds of construction. But this time there is something more to the noise. When I close my eyes and allow my mind to wash away the clamor of hammering, I can hear a delicate chitter of birdsong. I turn over in bed next to Nettie and listen to those *chirrup chirrup* sounds going on outside. I cannot recall hearing the birds sing since we came to Chicago. Had they gone away because of the fire and are finally returning? Or is there something in me that can just now hear them again?

I think of how Mother and I were up at this time every day in Peshtigo. How we'd go outside when the sky was that soft, ginger color of morning to milk our three goats and two cows. I remember her pointing out the tiny finches in our trees as we walked to the barn, saying, *"See those birds? Don't be fooled by their size. They may be small, but they are strong and can weather even the most terrible winter storms."*

"What kind of birds are they?" I asked.

"People call them common house finches, but there is nothing common about those birds. They are extraordinary when you think about it." Then she would take my hand and lead me into the barn. Most days, we worked in silence, but on occasion she would sing an old Irish song or ask about my schoolwork.

I slide out of bed and into my clothes. Those *twitter-chittering* finches outside Miss Franny's place make me want to get up and work. Make me—amazingly—want to remember Mother. Make me feel as if good things are coming.

So I'm not surprised when, later in the morning, Mr. Olsen stops his carriage in front of the boarding-house.

I am at the sink, washing the last few oatmeal bowls from breakfast when Nettie skips in and sings out, "Did you see who's here? Mr. Olsen!"

This is the first time he's been by since bringing Quinn and me to the boardinghouse.

"And just when I have to go to school," she says, her joy turning into a pout.

I skim the flecks of oatmeal from the wash water and put them in a bowl for the remaining hens.

"Look at his coat!" She is running into the front room, pressing her nose to the window and then skipping back and reporting the scene to me. "Have you ever seen anything so fine?"

She runs to the window again. "He has a bag. Oh Ailis, do you think there's something in it for us? Maybe he brought oranges . . . or jam?"

The front door opens and I can hear Miss Franny buzzing around him like a mosquito as they step into the house. *What a lovely surprise to see you, Mr. Olsen*, and *How's the railroad business going?* Her voice is like tinkling bells, like nothing I have ever heard come from her mouth before.

I shake my head and keep washing.

Nettie can't contain her excitement and says, "What's in the bag?"

Miss Franny looks to Nettie. "Shouldn't you be off to school?"

Mr. Olsen steps forward. "Muffins and apples and cream." He hands the bag to Nettie. "From my home to yours."

Nettie holds the bag tightly and tucks her nose down into the opening. "Are these muffins for all of us?"

Miss Franny takes the bag. "That's enough now, child. Off to school."

"There are two dozen muffins." He leans over and smiles at Nettie. "Plenty for all." Then he looks up and sees me across the way. "How are you faring today, Ailis?"

"Well, sir," I say.

Mr. Olsen reaches into his pocket and pulls out two small gray-white squares. "It's Mexican chicle gum," he says, holding the pieces out in his palm. "From the jungles of the Yucatán. Go on, take it."

Nettie goes first and grins widely as she bites into the gum. "It's not like the pinesap we usually chew—it's sweet!"

"Thanks to my friend Thomas Adams. This is his newest recipe. It'll be in stores everywhere within the next year but you, my dear, are one of the first American children to taste it."

"Try it, Ailis," Nettie says.

I take the chicle. "I'll save mine. Thank you, Mr. Olsen."

Miss Franny places the bag Mr. Olsen brought on the kitchen table. Then she gives Nettie a soft push from behind. "Grab your books."

Nettie takes her writing book and pencil from the table. "Yes, ma'am."

"And you, Ailis?" Mr. Olsen asks. "Are you off to school, too?"

Miss Franny hasn't allowed Quinn and me to attend school with Nettie and the other children in the neighborhood. She says we're too old to be going, but I know it is because she doesn't believe the Irish are worthy of an education.

"Ailis has been a wonderful help to me here," Miss Franny says before I can answer.

Mr. Olsen tilts his head. He is a broad man with a wide, friendly face and a short white beard. "That's good to hear," he says. "But are you implying the girl is not attending to her studies?"

Miss Franny sways her hips and brushes a hand along the table. "Well, I tried to get her to go, begged her almost. But she doesn't see the value in education as we do. I suppose it is the farm in her. She wasn't interested in her studies and I certainly couldn't force her."

"And her brother? Where is he?"

"Out back," I say, "putting new boards on the shed."

Miss Franny cuts her gaze to me, but I am feeling brave.

"Miss Franny is telling you the truth," I go on. "I tried to get out of schoolwork, but the longer I stay away, the more I realize my parents would be sad to know I quit going."

"Your father was an educated man," Mr. Olsen says. "I've no doubt his wish was for you to attend school."

"Yes, that was always his dream for us."

"Then you must go." Mr. Olsen is decisive.

"Both of them?" Miss Franny asks.

"Absolutely. I am paying you a wage to run this house and, while the children can be of some help, I certainly don't expect them to do it at the expense of their education."

I can almost see the frustration radiating from her but she manages to offer a constrained smile. "It was what the children wanted."

"It's all my fault," I say, going over to Nettie's side. "But I will listen to your wisdom now, Mr. Olsen, and tell my brother we must attend school, starting today."

"Hooray!" Nettie shouts with a jump.

"Take a muffin with you," he says.

I start for the bag, but think better of it when I catch the look on Miss Franny's face. "It's fine," I say. "We're late already." I don't give Mr. Olsen a chance to make Miss Franny any angrier. I just grab Nettie's hand and pull her out the door.

"I want a muffin," she says on the back step. "They smell good and I accidentally swallowed that chicle gum."

"You can have a muffin later." I turn to Quinn, who stopped hammering when we came out. "Mr. Olsen thinks we should go to school."

"And he gave us candied gum," Nettie says.

Quinn puts a nail up against the last new board. "I'm not going to school."

"Just come," I say. "And do it now."

"Everyone will laugh at me," he says, raising the hammer and driving the nail through the board in two swift swings. Quinn is young, but digging irrigation ditches and hauling bushels in the cranberry bogs have made him strong.

"Please, Quinn," I say, hoping Mr. Olsen won't leave before we get out of Miss Franny's range. "I need you to come with us."

Quinn looks at me and understands. He has always been good at reading into my words. "All right," he says, setting the hammer down. "I'm coming."

• • •

Nettie is crushed when I tell her Quinn and I aren't really going to school.

"But you promised Mr. Olsen," she says.

"We will still be getting an education. It's just going to have to be less structured, that's all."

"By taking a job?"

I bend down on one knee, looking at Nettie. "Listen, you have to keep this a secret for us. Once Quinn and I find work, we can save up and move into a nice place where we're welcome. All three of us together."

"Like a real family?" Nettie asks, rubbing her hand under her nose.

"With bedtime stories and songs around the fireplace—the whole picture."

She considers what I've said. "Do you think Miss Franny will be sad if we leave? What if she misses us?"

"Miss Franny will be happy to have three less people in her house."

"And Mr. Olsen," Nettie says, her hand rubbing again. "What will he think?"

"Mr. Olsen is a busy man. He will be glad to know we are taking care of ourselves." Then I cinch it. "Listen, Nettie, the state of Illinois won't pay for your boarding forever. They'll rebuild the orphanage and back you'll go. All alone again."

Her mouth falls open. "Do you think so?"

"Don't you remember that cook telling you they were already rebuilding the orphanage?"

"Charlie did say that."

"Once it is finished you'll have to go. Quinn and me finding work is our only chance to be together."

"Okay, Ailis," Nettie says as she pokes out her little finger. "I pinkie promise not to tell."

I wrap my pinkie around hers and look over to Quinn. "Come on," I say. "Put yours in."

Quinn rolls his eyes but then covers our pinkie fingers with his own.

"To the grave," I say in my most somber voice. Then I kiss our hands to seal the promise.

"Ewww," Quinn says, pulling his hand back.

"My lips didn't even touch you," I say, defensive. "I purposely kept them on my side."

"They were close enough."

Nettie giggles.

"All right," I say, "you go to school, Net, and we will meet you here at this buckeye tree at three o'clock." I point to a tree on the corner.

Nettie agrees and skips off to school while Quinn and I turn north, toward downtown Chicago. The fire started in the O'Learys' barn and spread mostly northeast. I saw the edges of the destruction when we were brought down from Peshtigo, but I haven't seen the worst of it. Even with weeks of rebuilding, the city is a mess of rubble. Everywhere we look, we see piles of rocks and shapeless brick mounds that were once prosperous businesses and vibrant homes.

The great city of Chicago is nothing but a blistered skeleton.

We walk on in a shocked-but-kind-of-curious way,

through the charred streets. The only people we see are those either hauling rubble out or carting loads of new lumber in.

"Where are they going to put all of this trash and debris?" I wonder out loud.

Quinn walks over to a man who is pushing a wheelbarrow that is piled high with charred wood scraps. "Excuse me, sir," Quinn says. "Who would we talk to about finding work?"

The man sets down the wheelbarrow, pulls a handkerchief from his shirt pocket, and mops sweat from his forehead. "Teddy's the foreman for this job. You can apply over at city hall."

"What's a person get paid for carting rubble?"

"Depends," the man says. "A boy your size would probably earn in the neighborhood of five dollars a week."

"Thank you for your help," Quinn says.

The man tucks the handkerchief back into his pocket, picks up the wheelbarrow handles, and continues down the road.

"Should we go to city hall?" I ask Quinn.

"I'm not sure I want to haul rubble," he says. "And they're not going to hire a girl, that's for sure."

I know he's probably right so I say, "Let's go over to Canal Street. Sam was telling me tourists have come from all over the country to see this mess. He even said he saw a lady steal a burned sign from one of the fire stations."

"What for?" Quinn asks.

"As a souvenir of a nation's tragedy, I guess. If what he says is true, then there have to be places for those tourists to shop and sleep and eat. Some of those places must be hiring."

Quinn follows me as I walk back out toward the edge of the fire's path.

When we finally make it to the west end of Canal Street, I wave my arm and say, "Just like Sam told me." Here, people fill the streets and vendors set up makeshift stores wherever there is a bare spot of land. "This is closer to Miss Franny's anyway," I say. "Fifteen-minute walk, tops."

Quinn points to a hotel. "There's a sign in that window, maybe they're hiring."

"No," I say. "It just says they have rooms open. See the capital *V*? It reads, *Vacancy*, which means empty rooms. Don't feel bad," I say. "That's a hard word. We need to look for a sign that says *Help Wanted*. You can find the word *help*." He nods and keeps looking.

I have been thinking about what Mr. Sullivan said about the Irish being disliked and I know it's time to tell Quinn an important fact about our job search. "And when we apply for work, we have to change our names. I can still go by

Ailis because it's also an English name, especially if I change the spelling to A-l-i-c-e. But you'll have to drop Quinn. And Doyle is entirely too Irish."

"I'm not changing anything."

I need to be firm. "Yes, you are. I'm telling you, Quinn, Chicago doesn't want to hire us. Besides, it's only for when we're at work. Think of it as a sort of make-believe."

"What will I go by?"

"How about Steven. Steven and Alice Smith. And let me do the talking." Then I see it. A brick building on the corner with two signs. The first sign hangs over the door and reads, IDA MUENCH, MILLINER and the second leans against the window and reads, HELP WANTED.

I point to the shop. "They're hiring here, let's go."

Quinn steps back. "I'm not touching lacy things, no sir."

For a flash, I wonder how he knows it is a millinery shop, but then notice the window display full of hats, gloves, and a bright pink parasol with lace trim. "Maybe you can work in the storeroom. Let's at least ask." I pull the door of the shop open and a bell hanging from a cord above chimes. Quinn makes a face at the sound of that delicate bell. "We need this," I whisper to him.

The shop is overflowing with femininity. There are straw bonnets, crushed-velvet hats with feathers and silk trim, gathered lace veils bustled up with flowers . . . There is even a wall of parasols dangling in a row by thin string. I can't help but let out a sigh at the luxury of it all.

"Oh brother," Quinn says, just behind me.

Before I can shut the door an elderly lady comes out from the storeroom. "Yes?" She is short and thick and speaks with a German accent.

"We're here to inquire about your help-wanted sign," I say. "We're looking for work."

"We? You and your shadow?" she asks, peering around me.

"Me and my . . ." I turn to pull Quinn over to my side, but he is gone. "Just a moment," I say to the lady, leaning out the open door and looking up and down Canal Street.

Quinn is nowhere to be seen.

"You let the cold in," the woman says. "Come in or go out, which do you choose?"

I look once more for any sign of Quinn. "In," I say, stepping into the shop and closing the door behind me. "I need work. I'm dependable and a quick learner."

The woman inspects my appearance. I fold my hands over the largest of the stains on my skirt and smile, trying to appear friendly.

"Family?" she asks abruptly.

"Just my brother. We are staying at a boardinghouse owned by Mr. Olsen. Have you heard of him?"

She lifts a shoulder and lets out a puff of air. "Who hasn't?" Then she flicks a finger toward me and says, "Is that your only dress?"

"Yes, ma'am. We lost our parents and baby sister in Peshtigo's fire and we need to make a new life for ourselves." I don't know why I feel compelled to tell her that, but I suddenly want this job more than anything. "Please, I beg of you."

"Your dress will never do," she says. "The ladies who come into this shop expect a certain level of nicety."

"If you could give me an advance on wages, even a small one, I will buy a suitable dress."

"An advance?" Her gray eyebrows are raised. "You don't even have the offer and already you are asking for an advance? What is your name?"

"Alice Smith."

"Your real name, girl. I hold no malice for the Irish, which you clearly are. Your hair gives you away."

I reach up and touch my braid. "Doyle," I say. "Ailis Doyle."

"So you are in my employ for two minutes and already you ask for an advance of money and tell me a lie. Is this how it shall be?"

"No, ma'am." Then I realize what she said. "In your employ?"

"Why not? I have work to be done and there you are standing in my doorway. We will have to figure out what to do about your dress. I will give it some thought." She looks at me longer and says, "There is something about you that reminds me of myself as a young girl in Munich."

"My schoolteacher Mr. Frankel was from Munich!"

"See?" she says, sliding a pile of straight pins from the counter into a box. "It is meant to be."

5

Quinn is waiting at the buckeye tree with Nettie when I get there at three o'clock. "Where did you go?" I ask.

"I don't want to work in that shop." He takes Nettie's hand and starts down the street toward Miss Franny's.

"I was worried," I go on, trailing behind them. His walk is curt and deliberate and Nettie is nearly skipping to keep up with him.

I run past them and turn into their path, forcing him to stop.

"I'll never be able to save up enough for both you and Nettie on my own. If you don't work with me, we'll be stuck at Miss Franny's forever."

"Why should I cart rubble or work in a ladies' shop for

five dollars a week just to move out into another boarding-house that costs the same five dollars a week?" he asks. "It doesn't make any sense."

"We're going to move into a place where we are wanted and treated kindly," I answer.

"You're not thinking this through," Quinn says. "We're staying at Miss Franny's for free but we both know she charges five dollars a week. And that's about what someone will pay kids like us to work. So if you earn five dollars and I earn five dollars, we can both move out. But where does that leave Nettie? Even if that fancy shop pays you six or seven dollars a week, it still won't be enough."

"Then we will both work for three months and put our money aside. That will give us two months of rent for the three of us."

"And then what?"

"Fine, we will both work for *six* months and that will give us four months to figure out our next step."

"Well as long as you get what you want," Quinn says, tugging Nettie down the road again.

"What's that supposed to mean?" I ask, following them.

"It means I'm tired of doing what you tell me to." He is angry and something tells me it's about more than getting a job. That it's about my asking him to come to the store with me back on that day in Peshtigo and about how I made him stop at the fabric mill so I could look at the new calico prints they were making. And probably about how I pulled him into the Menominee River when he wanted to run through the flames and go home.

When we finally get to Miss Franny's, I tell Nettie to go inside, and then I turn to Quinn. "You couldn't have saved them," I say. "You would never have made it home." Then I keep going when I should just shut my mouth. "Have you forgotten how hot the fire was? How half the survivors staying at the church were blinded from the heat alone? Don't you remember walking home after the fire passed and seeing spun glass around the roots of the felled trees? How hot does it have to be to turn the sand on those roots into glass? You can blame me all you want, but I'll never be sorry for saving you. Or for saving myself."

"I have chores to do," he says, going over to the woodpile. He lifts the ax above a fat log and splits it in two.

I walk over to where he is. "I'll wither up inside if I have to live my life under Miss Franny's rule. And Nettie deserves a family. We need your help, Quinn. I'm going to work at the millinery shop and I need you to find a job as well."

"You're not listening," he says. "If I could find work that paid more than five dollars a week, I would. But if I get a job carting rubble or follow you into that hat shop, we'll still be stuck living here so what's the purpose?" He goes back to chopping. I know he's done talking so I leave him there with Miss Franny's woodpile.

Once inside, I make it a point to wash Miss Franny's floors right away. I am on my hands and knees, scrubbing under her long dining room table where all the boarders eat when I hear her come in.

"Humph," she says above me.

I dip the rag into the bucket and keep scrubbing, not looking up.

"And the porch needs a good sweeping," she says.

"Yes, ma'am."

"And someone needs to beat the dust out of the front room rug."

"I am happy to, Miss Franny," I say, focusing my rag on splattered gravy that is dried in a glop on one of the table legs. "I'll get to it shortly."

She says nothing, but I can feel her standing over me while I use my thumbnail to scratch at the brown glob of gravy.

"Don't take the finish off my table," she says sharply.

But then she is gone.

I sit back on my heels and smile. The sound of those birds singing in the trees this morning comes to mind, along with a whisper of Mother's voice: *See those birds? Don't be fooled by their size. They may be small, but they are strong and can weather even the most terrible winter storms. You can do this, Ailis Doyle.*

Sam is on the front porch when I finish scrubbing the floor and go out to sweep.

"I heard you went to school today," he says from his chair.

"Really?" is all I can think to say.

"Sure did," he says, leaning back in his chair. "Fran mentioned it. But I also heard you arguing with your brother about taking a job in town."

I stop sweeping. "Please don't tell anyone about the millinery shop. Miss Franny thinks she owns us and I need to start—"

He holds up a hand. "I left home when I was just thirteen. My pa was an accountant in New York City and expected me to follow his path. Can you see me sitting behind a desk?"

I look at Sam's broad shoulders, thick arms, and crooked nose—likely that way from one too many street fights. "No."

"Neither could I. So I packed what little I had and took off in the middle of the night."

"Without saying anything?"

"My pa wasn't interested in anything I had to say."

"Have you ever visited your family?"

"I might go someday, when the fidget is out of my bones," Sam says. "The only reason I said anything is because I've

54

learned a lot over these past fifteen years—much of it the hard way—and I was thinking there might be a few things I can teach you and Quinn."

"Like what?"

"Well, for starters, you should always keep your business private. No one needs to know what you have in your pocket or how it got there, understand?"

I nod, leaning against the broom.

"And it sounds like you've found good work but I understand what your brother is saying, too. Why don't you get him," Sam says. "I've got an idea he might like."

I go tell Quinn to come to the front porch. Sam reaches in his pocket, pulls out his harmonica, and starts playing. I have never met anyone who can work a harmonica like Sam. He puts a simple block of wood to his lips and pushes out a musical story. Sometimes it is jaunty and glad, sometimes it's filled with sorrow, but when Sam plays it feels like there's more than just music happening. It feels like he's telling you something.

"See this beauty?" Sam says, holding the instrument up. "She has put change in my pocket more times than I can count through the years."

Quinn is immediately interested. "Really?"

"Sure," Sam says. "Before I had my job at the iron smith, I relied solely on my harmonica and sometimes I still use it to earn extra pocket change. I just stand on a busy corner downtown, flip my hat upside down on the sidewalk, and play until the coins start rolling in. Of course, when I was young, they rolled in faster than ever. There's something about a child that makes people loosen their purse strings." He puts the harmonica to his mouth and plays a few bars before going on. "And the folks milling around Chicago have had their hearts softened by the fire. Maybe they survived it, or maybe they're poking around, gawking at those of us who did. Either way, it's prime picking for this type of work." He plays two more bars of a lighthearted tune. "If you take your fiddle down on Canal Street and play it like I heard you playing outside in the middle of the night, you'll do your part to help Ailis and Net."

"Can I earn more than the five dollars a week I'd get for filling carts with rubble?" Quinn asks.

"I wouldn't be surprised if you could," Sam says. "When you play that fiddle in the midnight hours, it pulls me from my sleep. Two nights ago it had me sitting on the edge of my bed thinking all sorts of thoughts I hadn't had in years. You've got heartache to share and talent to back it up. That's what makes people stop and listen."

Quinn has been playing Father's fiddle in the middle of the night?

Then Sam adds, "I've seen peddlers building fire pits out

of hammered steel on a few corners downtown. You could play by those to keep from getting cold. Or try the indoor bazaar on Clinton, just a block west of Canal Street. I wonder if you could ask a restaurant or hotel to let you play in their lobby as entertainment for their guests, too. Move around a bit. If people see you playing in the same spot every day, they'll be less likely to drop a coin."

"There was one of those fire pits next to a jerky cart, not far from the hat shop," I say.

"Makin' money just by playing," Quinn mumbles, still trying to believe it.

"Making *good* money," Sam says. "And making people happy. Remember that, too."

Quinn returns to the woodpile and once he is out of earshot I ask, "Do you really think he can do it?"

"Have you heard your brother play lately?"

"No, but I suppose he was getting pretty good back in Peshtigo."

"Going through what you both did changes people," Sam says. "And Quinn's been playing music to the chickens in the middle of the night because his heart is trying to make sense of it all. If he can help what's left of his family while still connecting to the part he lost, then there's a chance he'll be all right in the long run."

6

We find a fire pit on the corner next to Ketchum's Butcher Shop the next morning and Quinn says it's as good of a place as any to start playing.

"Move somewhere inside if you get too cold," I tell him, but the fire really is warm and the owner of the butcher shop seems happy to have entertainment at his door.

I leave Quinn tuning his strings and head a block over to the millinery shop.

Standing there, I say a two-part wish. The first part is that Miss Franny won't notice how I swiped one of her aprons from the nail on the kitchen wall and the second part is that the apron will cover enough stains on my dress to help it look presentable. Oh, and also that Quinn will have a good day playing the fiddle. So a three-part wish, I guess.

The bell over the door chimes as I come in and Mrs. Muench looks up from her work at the main counter. "Good," she says in her German accent, which makes the word sound more like *goot*. "You are on time." Then she notices the apron. "And I see you tried with the dress."

I run my hands down along Miss Franny's apron. It is a simple green print on a beige cotton background but it is clean and pressed. It is worlds better than my dress which, Mrs. Muench was right, is awful.

"Thank you, Mrs. Muench," I say. "I hope it's nice enough."

"It's not," she says curtly. "And call me Ida."

"My parents always taught me to speak to adults using the Mrs.—"

She waves a hand to cut me off. "I set the rules." Each syllable is sharp and short.

"Yes, ma'am."

"Yes, Ida?" she asks.

"Yes." I pause. "Ida."

"Now about that dress." She disappears into a rear doorway. As she leaves, the front door chimes and I turn to see two ladies coming in.

"Good morning," I say as I dip my chin. "May I help you?"

They look at me and then look at each other and I know Ida is right about my dress, apron or no apron.

"Is Ida in?" the taller of the two ladies asks. Her hat sports a royal blue feather that bounces as she speaks and I can't help but notice she has three chins that bobble and match the feather's bounce.

I turn to the doorway where Ida has gone. "She's in the back, but I am her new shopgirl. Can I be of any help?"

The bobbling-feather-and-chin lady looks me over once again and then seems to concede. "Can you please tell Ida Lady June is here to collect her new hat?"

It is clear she is putting on airs. *Lady* June, indeed. There are no *Lady*s in America. I offer another small bow and say, "But of course." I start toward the storeroom and run into Ida as she is coming out with a dress draped over her arm. "I remembered that I had this—" she starts to say before she notices the two ladies standing in her shop.

"Lady June has come to collect her new hat," I say, trying to sound professional.

"I have it ready for you." Ida puts the dress down on the counter and starts over to a hat rack in the corner, but Lady June steps in her way and gives her a concerned look.

"This girl said she works for you now. Is it true?" she asks.

"She started this morning."

"But she's . . ." Lady June doesn't finish her sentence. "Now, Ida, I am just being mindful of your reputation."

I can't stop looking at her feather and chins as she speaks.

"The girl may need a bit of polish," Ida says, "but she'll be fine. Let me get your new hat."

"You can't polish the Irish off of her," Lady June says, and a snicker escapes from the mouth of her friend, who is still standing by the front door.

Ida looks down at her feet and twists the toe of one shoe on a floorboard. Then she looks up with a broad smile and says, "Lady June, would you like your hat or not?"

"It is because I respect your work," Lady June says. "And I wouldn't want rumors to start."

"Because if you do not want your hat," Ida says, "I have another customer who was admiring it yesterday. A Mrs. Carlson, I believe."

I don't know who Mrs. Carlson is but it is clear that Lady June doesn't want her touching the hat. "No, no, I'll take it."

Ida turns to me and says, "Ailis, will you retrieve the yellow-and-white hat from the rack?" She stands like a rock wall behind me as I get the hat and wrap it up.

When Lady June and her friend leave, Ida mumbles, *"Dummkopf,"* which I remember Mr. Frankel saying whenever one of the boys misbehaved in school, so I know it isn't a compliment.

"I'm sorry to cause you trouble."

"No trouble. I am the only milliner left after the fire. There are charity events almost daily and these women don't want to be seen in the same outfit over and over. They insist upon new things and so they are stuck with me." She says that last part with a smug kind of smile. "For you," she says, picking the dress up and holding it out.

It isn't anything close to what Lady June or her friend were wearing, but it is still far nicer than anything I've ever owned. "Thank you." I run my fingers across the hem. It is light blue cotton with a line of cream lace that runs across the chest and up over the shoulders. "It's lovely."

"It used to be mine but that was many *Schokoladentorten* ago."

"What's a *Schoko* . . . ?" I try, but can't pronounce the word like she does.

"You would call it chocolate cake."

"Oh."

"I have others, too. I know it's silly of me to keep old dresses that have grown too small, but I couldn't bring myself to throw them out—and now, look, I've found a use for them."

"Would you mind if I kept it here and changed when I came each morning?"

"But I am giving this dress to you. To have always."

I don't want to sound ungrateful but I'm not sure how to

explain away the new dress to Miss Franny so I say, "Our boardinghouse is poorly kept and I would be worried about ruining it. You see what has happened to my dress."

Ida looks down at the stains on my skirt. "If you think it best."

I take the dress.

"What are you waiting for then?" she says, waving toward the storeroom. "Go change. There is much work to be done and too little time. Enough of this standing around, talking about nothing!"

Her words are sharp but they aren't like Miss Franny's.

They are entirely different.

• • •

Quinn is still in front of the butcher shop when I get off work. I walk up slowly and stand behind a large sign on the sidewalk advertising pork chops. *100% REAL PORK*, it reads and I wonder whatever in the world could be in pork chops otherwise?

Quinn looks so alone standing there with Father's fiddle case open at his feet. A woman pulling along a little girl brushes past me and stops in front of Quinn. The girl skips in place and swings her arms out in a dance, and the mother says to Quinn, "How old are you, boy?"

Quinn keeps playing but answers, "Eleven."

"Does your mother know where you are?"

"I don't have a mother. She died with my father and baby sister in Peshtigo's fire."

At that, the little girl stops her dance but Quinn smiles and says, "Here's a song for you," and then starts an even faster, lighter song that sounds like fairy feet sprinting through the forest. The girl giggles and begins skipping in place again.

"God bless you," the woman says when he is done. She pulls two bills from her black velvet bag and drops them into Quinn's fiddle case.

Bills!

Ida promised me one dollar and twenty-five cents per day and the ability to work only school hours plus Saturdays after my work is finished at the boardinghouse, which I think is generous. Quinn nearly doubles my daily pay in thirty seconds.

As the woman takes the girl's hand and walks off, I notice a broken piece of yellow chalk on the sidewalk where the girl had been dancing. I step out from behind the sign and come forward, picking up the chalk and sliding it into my skirt pocket. The girl is only one store down and I can easily return the chalk to her, but instead I wrap my fingers around it and hold it tightly.

"You're good," I say to Quinn.

"Not as good as Father."

"No, but he had played a lot longer. I bet you'll be as good as him someday."

Quinn adjusts one of the fiddle strings. "He doesn't seem so far away anymore."

"Who?"

"Father."

I think about the finch songs and know what he means. "How'd you do?" Then I notice there are only those two bills I saw the lady drop into the fiddle case. Quinn reaches down and picks them up. "Two dollars is still a lot of money," I say.

"There's more," he says. "I learned pretty quickly that people like to put their money in an empty case. I guess they feel more needed if no one else has dropped a coin. And they also feel like you have enough if they see others giving you something. So . . ." He reaches in his coat pocket and pulls out a handful of coins and bills.

"Put it back," I say, glancing down the street.

"What for?"

"Because I don't want to get robbed is what for. We'll count it later."

Quinn puts the money into his pocket. "I counted it as it came in. I made three dollars and thirty-seven cents, minus the twenty-five cents I spent on a sandwich and milk for lunch. Plus these two dollars makes five dollars and twelve cents. At this rate," he says, "you could go to school and not even have to work at that lady's shop."

"I don't want to go to school anymore."

"But you love school."

"I think Miss Franny is right. I'm too old for that nonsense."

Quinn shakes his head. "The Ailis I know would never call school nonsense."

"Well, I'm not that Ailis anymore." I keep my fingers locked around the yellow chalk in my pocket. "And maybe it's time for both of us to grow up."

7

I have been working at Ida Muench's millinery shop for two weeks when Lady June returns. She comes in the front door amid a flurry of snowflakes and wind, wearing a black wrap with red fur trim and a fully bustled red dress. It is an ordinary Tuesday morning, but she is decked out as if President Ulysses S. Grant might show up at any moment and invite her to tea. I am thankful to be wearing a pretty gray woolen dress Ida gave me with pleats around the skirt and velvet trim on the collar—but also mad at myself for caring. Ida is in the back, wrapping a piece of felt around a hat block, so I put down the parasol frame I am pulling out of a delivery box and step forward.

"Good morning, Lady June. Don't you look lovely?" Ida

taught me to compliment the ladies who come into the shop. They are there to buy image and vanity, she often reminds me, and will spend more if we boost their egos.

"Is Ida in?" She won't even look at me as she asks.

"Ida is working on a bonnet at the moment and cannot be interrupted. May I be of assistance?"

Lady June pulls off her black gloves one finger at a time and then lines them up and begins flipping them against one hand. She lets out a loud sigh and says, "I suppose," as if having me assist her is the biggest imposition of her life. "It goes without saying I will be attending the Chicago Aid Society's gala this Saturday afternoon."

"It wouldn't be a proper event without you."

She stops flipping her gloves and looks at me, maybe deciding if I am being sarcastic or not. "Quite," she says.

I find myself watching her chins and feeling a bit disappointed that she is wearing a basic spoon bonnet without a feather to bounce along. It is far less entertaining.

"And I have the need for a new parasol to reveal when I arrive at the gala. All of Europe is sporting parasols these days. They are a symbol of class and ideal femininity."

"So I've heard. Tell me, what did you have in mind?"

"Something fresh and different. Something that will set me apart from the ladies who somehow finagle an invitation, but really have no business being there."

"And who have no idea what proper fashion is," I add.

She gives me another look but then seems to decide I am being serious. "You understand."

"Oh, I do, and I also understand how a person's reputation can be destroyed if she shows up with the wrong accessories. Accessories are what make a quality citizen, after all." I worry I have gone too far but Lady June only nods in agreement.

"Ida has taught you well."

I am struck by how ridiculous this conversation is—especially given the post-fire environment of the city and the fact that this gala is meant to raise money for the needy. I doubt the families who huddle under the bridges at night, freezing and starving, care about what kind of lace is on Lady June's parasol.

Lady June continues, "And don't show me anything remotely close to what has already been sold to other ladies who might be attending."

"Then I will put aside this special piece from Spain that was requested by Mrs. Carlson." I am amazed at how quickly this idea and Mrs. Carlson's name came to mind. I have not yet met her, but remember the name from my first encounter with Lady June. "Something she said her husband saw the queen of Spain carrying on his latest business trip to Europe," I say.

"John Carlson went to Europe? And met the queen of Spain? But his business is not international."

"That's a new development," I say, not even feeling bad for what I am doing. "It's a secret."

Lady June's chins quiver as she nods briefly and whispers, "I won't breathe a word."

"Anyway," I continue, "I guess all of Europe is talking about how fashionable the Spanish queen is, with her new style of parasol, and Mrs. Carlson insisted she have one exactly like it for this Saturday's gala. Of course, she hasn't actually paid for it, so I suppose it is technically still for sale."

"Show it to me at once."

I go over to the box we just received from our distributor that is full of the skeleton frames for parasols. Ida explained to me how the parasol frames are sent from New York and we stretch the fabric and lace across them to make a finished product. I pull out a simple wooden frame without a stitch of fabric on it, open it up, and twist it playfully on my shoulder. "Isn't it lovely?"

Lady June's mouth hangs open. "But there is nothing to it. It's an unfinished frame."

I shrug. "I guess that's fashion. I don't really understand it, either."

"I never said I did not understand fashion." I can see Lady June is getting worked into a lather, as Father used to say.

"Of course you didn't, Lady June. I was just thinking a more traditional style of parasol might be a good choice for you. Maybe something like this Chantilly lace one we have hanging from the ceiling. Everyone is wearing Chantilly lace. Some say it has become common, but I think it's beautiful. Don't you?"

"I have four Chantilly lace parasols already," she says, as if I should somehow know that.

"See? You do know what is in style." I go behind the counter and begin wrapping the parasol frame in paper. "I'll just set this aside for when Mrs. Carlson comes in this afternoon."

"I'll take it," Lady June says, though she sounds uncertain.

"But it was ordered for—"

"You did say that since it has not yet been paid for, it is technically still for sale, correct?"

I run a hand along the end of the frame. "Yes." I know what I am doing is wrong, and that Ida would be upset, but I can't seem to stop myself. Lady June thinks I am nothing, just because I'm Irish. And there's something about how she flaunts her opinions that angers me.

"Then I'll take it." This time she sounds more certain of her decision. "Oh, how thrilling it will be to see the look on Marie Carlson's face when I make my appearance."

"I have no doubt you'll be the talk of the town," I say.

"How much is it?"

"One dollar, seventy-five."

"But that's the same price as a parasol that has fabric on it."

"That's true," I say. "But you are also buying the guarantee that we won't sell another parasol like this to anyone else, and Mrs. Carlson is going to be so disappointed. Besides, it was imported and the wood is a rare Spanish oak." I honestly have no idea if such a thing even exists, but it sounds impressive.

"Give it here, girl."

"Yes, ma'am," I say, wrapping a navy silk bow around the paper. Lady June drops her money on the counter, takes the umbrella frame, and hurries out the door. She has only been gone for a minute when Ida comes in from the storeroom.

"Was there a customer?"

"Lady June bought a parasol."

"Splendid." Ida walks over to the counter and begins sorting pins into a box. "My late husband, Gunther, used to laugh at our store and say we sold everything that rendered a woman useless."

I smile, thinking about the completely worthless parasol Lady June just purchased and say, "He sounds like a smart man."

• • •

Quinn always plays to the end of his song when I arrive to pick him up once I am finished at work. I don't mind. It gives me a chance to hear him, even for a minute.

He is playing at the bazaar today and I am intrigued by his hands. One runs the bow over the strings and the other moves along the fiddle's neck, finding just the right note. His hands have never been soft because farming doesn't allow for that—but they are still young. Today they seem larger. Stronger. A miniature version of Father's, and looking at them makes me feel sad and think of precious Gertrude and her soft hands, which would get grimy from dipping them in the milk bucket before she petted our cows, Bonnie and Abigail. I wonder if Quinn ever thinks of Gertrude.

We don't talk about what happened in Peshtigo. We didn't even talk about what we were seeing as we saw it. We just walked side by side and took it all in and, by some means, ended up at the church and eventually in Mr. Olsen's carriage on our way to Chicago. It's all a blur really, and I can't honestly say what is a true memory anymore and what is from the terrible dreams that often trouble my sleep.

"How'd it go?" I ask once Quinn stops playing and is putting the fiddle in the case.

"Slow. I only made a dollar and fifty cents."

"That's still more than I made and it is all adding up to something good. Hurry, school is getting out and Nettie will be waiting."

He flips the latch on the case shut and stands up. "She's going to want to talk to that bird again, isn't she?"

"Probably."

And he is right. Nettie insists we stop by and visit Kristina, as she does most days.

Quinn fidgets out at the street while Nettie and I go into the yard to see the chicken. The McGintys don't know why Nettie has taken an interest in one of their hens, but they don't seem to mind when we stop by.

"It's starting to snow again," Quinn hollers at us from the road.

Nettie crouches down next to Kristina, who is digging in the dirt and ignoring her completely. She strokes the chicken's head with her pointer finger and carries on a one-sided conversation about how things are going in the coop at Miss Franny's and asking if Kristina is getting along with her new chicken family. I know to hang back a few feet. Kristina still doesn't like me much and it is Nettie's time with her anyway.

After a few minutes, Nettie stands up, turns to me, and says, "Kristina forgives you."

"For saving her life? How very nice."

Nettie smiles and shoves her hands into her coat pockets. "Yep," she says. "That's the kind of chicken she is. Nice."

When we return to Quinn he says, "Let's go already. It's really starting to snow and I'm freezing."

"Okay, okay," I say.

"I'm the one standing outside in the cold all day," he goes on. "I want to get warm for once."

I give him a look. Nettie knows we are both working, but we haven't told her exactly where we go each day because I don't want to put her in a position where she might accidentally slip and tell someone. She only knows we are both learning a lot and getting things ready for when we can move out of Miss Franny's place and find one of our own. That's all she needs to know and I don't want Quinn shooting his mouth off.

"Why are you outside all day, Quinn?" Nettie asks, as I knew she would.

"Never mind him," I say. "He just likes to complain."

Quinn stops walking. "*I'm* the one who complains?"

I pull on his sleeve. "Come on, I'll boil some water for tea. That'll warm you up."

"Miss Franny doesn't like to share her tea," Nettie says. "Or her cocoa."

"Then we'll have plain water," I say. "At least it will be warm."

But when we get back to the boardinghouse and no one is looking, I pinch some sugar into the mugs. It looks like plain water so Miss Franny can't say anything, but it tastes so sweet.

"Mmmm," Nettie says when she sits down at the kitchen table and sips her cup.

"It's magical water," I whisper. "I made it with a wish."

"A candy wish," Nettie whispers.

Quinn rolls his eyes and turns sideways in his chair, looking off into the front room, but I notice he drinks every drop.

8

The next morning it is still snowing, which makes me feel gloomy. People describe snow as soft and light and airy. Delicate even. They sing songs about snowflakes flitting through the air and landing gently on noses. It's easy to get caught up in these false ideas, especially if you've never had to live and work in true winter conditions. The truth about snow is that it's as heavy as a brick and can make your life miserable when it wants to.

Mother used to worry about the snow every time it started. I guess it came from a situation when I was just a baby. There was a blizzard so fierce that, no matter how much Father tried to shovel it away from the house, he couldn't keep up with it. The snow didn't stop for five days straight and by the time it did, we were completely snowed in. It was so deep it covered our door and all of our windows. The only thing allowing us to breathe was the chimney, which poked up out of the top of all those feet of white powder. Mother said we lost our livestock and nearly starved to death. Ever since then she warned me not to be fooled by the pretty appearance of falling snow. Wisconsin snow, she said, is nothing like the stuff people sing about. It is mindless and heartless. In fact, snowy days were the only times she ever talked about going back to Ireland.

When I come into the kitchen, I hear a shovel scraping against the front steps and know it is Quinn. Miss Franny has taken to working us for an hour or two before school as well as the five after. Mr. Olsen may have negotiated our freedom during school hours but she is getting nearly a full day's work from us all the same.

"Will you make a snowman with me, Ailis?" Nettie asks, running her finger against the inside of her bowl to get the last gummy piece of oatmeal.

"I have to grind the wheat for bread," I say. "I don't have time for a snowman."

"Not even a little snowman?"

I sit down next to her and rest my head on the table. It is exhausting to work for Ida and still try to keep Miss Franny happy. "And I have to do all the breakfast dishes. Besides, I hate the snow."

My head is down and my eyes are closed so I don't see Nettie's face, but I hear her suck in her breath. "You shouldn't hate anything," she says. "Sister Baldwin says hate kills your heart as fast as a wink."

Nettie likes to quote the nuns from her orphanage from time to time. Especially when I am tired and thin on patience.

"I bet Sister Baldwin has never been snowed in and almost died from starvation. Or lost all of her animals because her barn roof collapsed from the weight of the snow. Or got her wagon stuck in a drift, making her walk three miles home. I've experienced all of those things and, believe me, it's no picnic."

I keep my head down because, even though Nettie is silent, I know she has a look on her face and I don't want to see that look just now.

"Okay, Ailis," she says after a minute. "You don't have to."

I feel awful and consider going outside with her, but Miss Franny comes into the kitchen and starts slamming things around saying, "I'm glad you feel so relaxed, sleeping when this kitchen needs so much work."

I take Nettie's bowl and spoon and get started on the breakfast dishes.

And when my morning work is done and both Quinn and Nettie are waiting for me, we say goodbye to Sam (who takes over the shoveling) and head down the street.

We get about three houses away before our shoes are soaked through.

"Jump on my back," I say to Nettie.

But Quinn says he has a better idea and hands me his fiddle before returning to the boardinghouse for a shovel. "I'll walk ahead and push the snow aside with this shovel and you both can follow single file behind."

"Miss Franny won't like it," Nettie says, rubbing her hand under her nose.

"Miss Franny has two shovels," Quinn assures her. "So she won't notice if one is missing. I'll keep it safe with me and return it when we come home this afternoon. She can't get mad if she doesn't know about it."

"And we're doing a service for the city of Chicago by shoveling some of their snow," I add. "It's a good deed."

Nettie slows her hand and then puts it in her coat pocket with a solid nod, which Quinn takes to mean she agrees with his plan. And so he starts out ahead of us, pushing the snow aside in mounds as he goes down the street.

Before long, other children on their way to school join our line—one by one, with their mothers or aunties or whoever waving at Quinn from their porches like he is the cleverest boy in the world. Nettie walks right behind him and me behind her. She is lifting her knees in a marching sort of way and swinging her arms and the words come to my mind, *Nettie is a precious soul.*

• • •

It is still snowing at three o'clock when Quinn and I go to meet Nettie at the buckeye tree.

She is nowhere to be seen.

"Maybe she's waiting somewhere else," Quinn says. "These trees all look the same in winter."

"She has found the right tree every day until now. She knows where it is."

"Maybe she stayed after school."

My stomach starts turning around on itself. "Maybe."

We walk over to the barn that the city converted into a make-do schoolhouse until a new one can be built, but it is locked and no one is around.

"She's probably back at Miss Franny's," Quinn says.

I pull on the barn door again, hoping it will somehow slide open and reveal Nettie staying after school to sweep the floor or wash down the blackboard. That's the kind of thing she'd do. "Nettie!" I holler.

"I know!" Quinn says. "She's talking to that chicken."

"You're right." We take off in a sprint.

But when we get to the McGintys', our lungs burning from running in the cold snow, we find the hens huddled in their coop, alone.

I make Quinn wait by the buckeye tree while I go up and down the street, asking everyone who comes by if they have seen a girl with brown braids and a huge smile, dressed in a beige coat.

A couple of people know who Nettie is, but no one I talk to has seen her recently.

My heart is beating in a *thumpity, thumpity, thumpity* panic-skip sort of way but, as I walk toward Quinn, it slows down and falls into a heavy *thud, thud, thud.* Quinn reaches out and takes my hand. "She's waiting at Miss Franny's for us." He says it like it's true but we both know it isn't.

"You're late." Miss Franny is in a huff when we come in the back door.

"We were looking for Nettie," I say. Then, to cover our working situation I add, "She disappeared from the school yard while Quinn and I were inside. Is she here?"

Quinn comes in behind me, after sneaking Miss Franny's shovel into her shed, along with his fiddle.

"No," Miss Franny says, "and you should be chopping the onions." She points a finger toward a burlap sack in the corner.

"You're not listening to me. Nettie has gone missing. We can't find her anywhere and it's starting to get dark outside."

"Because it's late," Miss Franny says. "We have a houseful of boarders expecting dinner soon and you're off looking for a nothing girl who is likely playing in the streets or singing to stupid chickens."

"How can you say something so awful?"

Quinn pulls on my hand and I know he is warning me against my temper.

"Nettie!" I holler, pulling away from Quinn and searching the house. When I get to our room I see that the blanket on the bed is neatly folded and the sheets are stripped off. I turn and stomp into the kitchen where Miss Franny is pulling out a stack of tin plates for dinner. "What did you do with her?"

"I have no idea what you're talking about."

"You must have done something because the bed is all stripped down."

Miss Franny sets the plates on the table and flings her arms in the air. "Now I can't even wash my own sheets? Do the laundry in the boardinghouse I am charged to manage? So ungrateful, this one!" She turns to Quinn on that last part as if he will tell her she is right, but he just stands there. She drops her arms and says, "Useless, both of you!"

I storm out of the house, slamming the back door behind me. Quinn comes out quietly right after.

"She's never stripped off the sheets before," I say to him.

"Maybe you just never noticed," Quinn says. "Maybe she really was doing laundry."

"Miss Franny's behind this, I know it."

"What would Miss Franny have to gain from hurting Nettie?" Quinn asks.

I don't have a good answer for that. "I don't know," is all I can think to say.

Quinn sighs and pulls his coat closed in the front. He looks up to the sky, which has finally stopped spitting snowflakes, and says, "Let's start searching." It is the best thing he could have said.

We go down the street, knocking on every door and calling out Nettie's name. When Miss Franny's street has been checked, we move on to the next street and the next after that. After several hours, people quit answering their doors and Quinn says they are all in bed for the night.

We wander around through yellow spots of lamplight and patches of darkness and end up at the tall line of walnut trees by the community garden.

"Nettie!" I holler out once more, my voice cracking at the end.

"We'll look again tomorrow," Quinn says.

I lean up against a tree and drop my head into my hands. "She didn't even have good shoes on."

"It's pointless to search when everyone is asleep," Quinn says. "Let's go back, I'm freezing."

My feet went numb at least two hours before and the tips of my ears ache from the cold, but thinking about it only makes me worry about Nettie more. Only makes me think about how little she is and how the coat she was given from the church's donation box is more the fall type and not really the middle-of-December type and how she might be twice as cold as Quinn and I put together. Not to mention hungry. And scared. She must be terrified, wherever she is.

I shake my head. "I can't give up."

"We're not giving up, we're just saying it's too late right now."

I ignore Quinn and start wandering again. "Nettie!" I holler over and over, wondering if she's hurt and can hear us from wherever she is but just can't answer. At least then she'll know we are trying.

I am so distressed I don't even notice Sam until he is standing right in front of me.

"Ailis," he says, and I smell the bitter malt of ale on his breath. The pub must have just closed. "What are you two doin' out here at this hour?"

"Nettie's missing. We've looked everywhere. I think Miss

Franny did something . . . Maybe she threatened her and Nettie ran off, I don't know. But Nettie's gone and we can't find her."

"Why would Fran do something like that?"

"Because she's the devil!"

Sam pulls me in to his side. "Now, there," he says, and leans on me more than I am leaning on him. "That Franny's a tough bird, but she wouldn't hurt Nettie."

"How can you say that?" I ask. "What do you see in a person like her?"

Sam sways and says, "There's all kinds of beautiful in this world," and I know he is a lot more drunk than I originally thought. "Let's get you two home," he mumbles as his knees start to buckle. Quinn swoops in on the other side, helping me hold Sam up. He leans heavily on us and keeps mumbling about how he is getting us home but, really, it is Quinn and I who are struggling to lead him back through the frozen streets.

When we get to Miss Franny's, Sam stands up and tucks his shirt front into his trousers. Then he straightens Quinn's coat collar.

"Looking presentable and all of that stuff," he says before staggering up to the porch and swinging the front door wide open. "Darling!" Sam shouts into the dark house.

"She's going to kill him," I say, but Quinn shakes his head as we follow him up onto the porch.

"No. He comes back drunk like this all the time. She'll make him coffee and help him to his room."

I wonder what other things Quinn sees sleeping in the front room. Things none of us other boarders have any clue about.

An oil lamp flickers on inside, illuminating Sam propped up against the door frame. Golden light shines through his blond curls and from where I stand he looks like some sort of angel.

Miss Franny tightens the sash on her robe and tucks her head under Sam's arm, lifting him away from the door frame. "Come on, you," she says.

"I brought the little ones." Miss Franny must have thought it was the ale talking because she starts to pull the door shut, but Sam reaches his hand out, stopping the door, and says it another way. "Ailis and Quinn. I brought them home."

She notices me and Quinn standing behind Sam.

"I thought you both had run off, too. Did you find the sick girl?"

"No," Quinn says.

"Well, we had a need for her room and it's been rented. You'll both have to sleep on the floor." Then she goes back to tending Sam.

I turn to Quinn. "We didn't tell Miss Franny that Nettie was gone until just a few hours ago. How could she have rented the room so soon?"

Quinn shrugs and walks inside but I can't seem to make my feet move.

"It's late. Let's get some sleep," Quinn says, turning to me. And even though I'd much rather keep searching for Nettie, I follow him.

9

The new boarder is a scrawny old man with teeth so yellow they are almost orange. Quinn and I watch him from the kitchen. He plops down at the dining room table and scoops more than his fair share of the oatmeal into his bowl. Then he turns to smile at me and swipes four pieces of toast from the pile. He gives me the creeps and I make a wish that he will move along soon.

"I honestly can't believe Miss Franny rented that room so fast," I say after the man leaves the table. "How does she know Nettie won't be back?"

"It's not even a room, it's a closet," Quinn says. Then he lowers his voice and adds, "She dumped our other things in the shed, but our money is still there in that candle."

It is an excellent hiding place—a fat pillar candle Quinn hollowed out from underneath. When it stands on the shelf, it looks just like any other candle, but it is really a mini-bank that holds two and a half weeks of earnings. And that piece of sunshine-yellow chalk the girl on the street left behind.

"Maybe we should just leave it where it is," Quinn says. "For now."

"I don't trust that man. He'll pick the room clean of anything that's not nailed down before he checks out. Did you see him with the oatmeal?"

Quinn agrees. "You're right. But where else can we hide it?"

I stack the bowls that are on the counter, preparing to wash them. "Let me bring it to the hat shop. There are shelves in the storeroom that haven't been touched for years. Ida won't notice an extra candle."

"You're going to work today?"

There is a heavy lump in my chest, weighing my words down. "I thought about it all night and I can't risk losing my job. But I will ask Ida if I can get off work at two o'clock today so we can visit Nettie's schoolteacher before she leaves, and Father Farlane. I'm hoping they'll have some ideas."

Quinn places two dirty spoons side by side on the counter next to the bowls and asks, "What if she's gone, Ailis? What if we never find her?"

"Don't talk like that. We just need to think like Miss Franny and figure out how she could benefit from this situation. Then we'll know what she did with Nettie."

"Wasn't the state paying for Nettie's boarding?" Quinn asks. "Wouldn't she lose money by making Nettie leave? I really don't think Miss Franny is behind this."

I know Quinn is probably right but there is part of me that simply doesn't trust her. "Help me with these dishes," I say.

Just then, Miss Franny comes inside through the back door. Her gray shawl is wrapped up around her head and is spotted with snowflakes and I wonder where she has gone so early in the morning. "New day, new wood for the fire," she says to Quinn. That is her lousy way of asking him to please chop a pile before going to school.

"Yes, ma'am." He pulls his coat off the nail and goes outside.

"I have already ground the wheat and churned the cream into butter," I say, offering a submissive bow.

She looks over to where I have the wheat flour in a wooden bowl. "And you've made quite a mess with it, I see."

There is one tiny area of flour powder on the edge of the bowl, but the table and floor are perfectly clean. "Sorry," I say, taking a finger and carefully brushing the flour into the bowl.

"The chickens won't lay again if eggs remain in their nests," she quips.

"I have gathered the eggs and placed them in the basket. I also cleaned out the henhouse straw."

That surprises her. She leans over, looking out the window toward the henhouse. "How many eggs were there?"

"Four."

"How am I expected to feed ten people with four measly eggs? You and the boy will have to go without."

Is she really blaming me for there being only four eggs? I feel a pulse of anger rise up, but shake it off. "I also dusted the front room."

"When?"

"I was too worried about Nettie to sleep."

"I hope you didn't wake my *paying* customers by stomping around like some thoughtless elephant."

I remember Mr. Frankel teaching us about how elephants are as compassionate as humans—how they suffer from depression and even cry when they lose loved ones. "No, ma'am, I was careful to be quiet."

She unwraps her shawl, hangs it on a nail, and says, "Are those breakfast dishes still dirty?"

"I was just about to get water from the pump." Then I add, "But I will have them done before school."

We stand there for a moment, looking at each other.

"What are you gawking at?" she finally says, and I know that is as close to a thank-you as I'll ever get from Miss Franny.

At least she isn't screaming at me.

• • •

Ida has her head down as I come into work.

"Morning," I say, rushing by her toward the storeroom. Quinn recovered the candle from Nettie's room when the boarder was in the outhouse. I have it tied up in a square of cotton, trying to make it look like my lunch bundle.

"No running in the shop," she says. As I pass by her, I notice she is sewing red berries onto a navy blue hat, looping thread in circles around each berry.

I slow to a swift walk. "Sorry."

"I'm glad it has finally stopped snowing," she says as I go into the back. "Better weather, better business."

I pull a chair from the corner over to a single shelf that runs above a window. When I untie the square of cotton, I see that our money has spilled out. "Oh no," I mumble as I turn the candle upside down and begin shoving coins and bills into its hollow middle.

"I placed your dress on the railing," Ida says from the front.

"Thanks!" I say, grabbing at a nickel that has escaped and is rolling on its side across the floor.

"It's the plaid one."

"Okay."

Then her voice is close. "What are you doing?"

I look up and see Ida standing in the doorway.

With a wad of bills in my hand, it seems pointless to make something up. "We've been saving our money to get a place of our own, but now Nettie's gone," is all I can manage before my throat closes off.

Ida has me sit in the chair and then drags another one over. "You tell me everything," she says.

And even though Sam warned me against sharing personal information with others, I start at the beginning with how we came to Miss Franny's and how Nettie shared her room with me. I tell her about the way Miss Franny treats us and go all the way through Quinn and me working to earn our way into a better living situation and, finally, Nettie's troubling disappearance.

When I share the last detail, Ida clicks her tongue and says, "Poor child."

I don't know if she is talking about Nettie or about me, but it doesn't matter. Nettie and I are both in a horrible mess.

"You should not be with that woman," Ida says. "Perhaps

you and Quinn could come live with me. It is not fancy, but you will be safe and warm."

Ida lives in a tiny one-room apartment on the second floor of the four-story building where her shop is. I consider the offer, but her apartment is too small and I hate the thought of crowding her space, especially when she has been so kind. Besides, if we leave the boardinghouse, we might not figure out what happened to Nettie.

"We can't," I say, and she seems to understand. "I need to keep an eye on Miss Franny. Maybe I can learn something about what she did."

"If it is indeed her who did anything," Ida says.

"Right."

Ida wraps her arms around me and pulls me in to her soft, round shoulders. "So much trouble for someone so young." And then she adds, "Where is God in these moments?"

And I love her for saying that.

She holds me close for a while and then helps me put the last of the money into the candle. "You can trust me to keep this safe."

I thank her and then ask if I can leave at two o'clock so we can keep looking for Nettie.

"Go now," she says. "I'll take care of things here."

"What about the shipment coming from New York?" I ask. "Don't I need to help unpack the boxes?"

"Who cares about boxes when there is a child missing?"

"Are you sure?"

"I have been running this business for forty-seven years. I can manage."

"Thank you, Ida!" I say, already halfway to the front door. "Thank you!" I run all the way to the bazaar where Quinn is playing his music. "Ida gave me the day off," I tell him.

"I haven't been able to play anyway," he says, putting his fiddle into the case.

"Too worried?" I ask. The crease across his forehead tells me I am right.

He flips the two latches, locking the case, and says, "She's only six. She can't even fight for herself."

"Not that she'd try," I say.

School is still in session so we decide to start at the church.

Father Farlane isn't what I expect. He looks about the same age as Sam and Miss Franny and is one of those happy people with high, round cheeks and an easy smile. He invites us down a narrow hallway to his office.

"Sit, please." He motions to a bench beside his desk.

We explain about how Nettie didn't come home and that we are concerned something has happened to her.

"I know the girl," Father Farlane says, leaning back in his

chair and pressing his fingers into a steeple. "She loves candles and would light all of them if I didn't remind her to leave a few for other parishioners."

"That's Nettie," Quinn says.

Father Farlane continues, "She likes to sit with some of her friends from the orphanage."

I didn't know Nettie met other children at church, but it makes sense. They grew up together. No wonder she never misses a Sunday. It is a chance to see old friends. "Do you know who? Maybe they know something," I ask.

"I can't recall names. One has red curls and another is blond," he says, thinking. "And then there's that gentleman who came last week and sat with them. I was glad to see an adult watching over the children."

"What did he look like?" Quinn asks.

"Oh, large of stature, bald on top." Father Farlane rubs his hand along his head.

"Charlie?"

"Never got his name," Father Farlane says. "But they seemed happy to see him."

"He was their cook at the orphanage," I say.

"Is there anything more you can tell us?" Quinn asks.

"I'm sorry, there isn't. With so many churches damaged in the fire, my congregation has tripled. It's difficult to keep track of everyone and their situations." And then he says something that almost knocks me off my seat. "There was a woman who came asking about Nettie earlier this morning."

"What woman?" I ask.

"The mistress of the boardinghouse where the girl resides. Or did reside, I suppose."

"Miss Franny?" Quinn and I say in unison.

"That's right."

"What did she want?" I ask in shock.

"She inquired if I had seen the girl and asked me to be in touch if I came across any information. I'm glad to know Nettie has so many people looking for her and am certain she will turn up soon." He stands up and swings an arm out, showing us to the door. His black robe sways with the movement. As I pass him, he says, "I'll add her name to the prayer roll."

We go back down the narrow, dark hallway and out into the day.

"Why would Miss Franny talk to Father Farlane?" Quinn asks, shielding his eyes as they adjust to the light. Sun is breaking through the layer of clouds, making the snow gleam.

"Maybe she's covering her tracks," I say. "Trying to play the part of the concerned guardian."

"No, I think she really is concerned," Quinn says. "Remember how she came into the kitchen this morning covered with snow? She must have been out looking for Nettie."

I think about that. "But if Miss Franny didn't chase Nettie away, who did?"

"Let's go to the police," Quinn says. "They're supposed to help find runaways."

"I guess we should," I say, knowing they won't help. The city of Chicago is operating on a thread. With all that is going on, why would they care about one orphan girl gone missing?

"We also need to find that Charlie guy," Quinn says. "Maybe Nettie told him something."

When Quinn says those words, I remember Charlie's perfectly polished blue-black shoes with their oversize silver buckles. Shoes too nice for an out-of-work cook. I think about how friendly Charlie was with Nettie and I realize there are chunks of her day when she is away from us and that we have no idea who she talks to or spends time with.

Later, after we finish the last of our chores, Quinn falls asleep next to me in Miss Franny's front room and I say a prayer. I can't bring myself to pray to God, but I curl my knees up under my blanket, tip my chin down, and ask Mother and Father for help. I ask them to make the police care enough to try (they took a report halfheartedly and told us they couldn't make any promises). I ask them to bless

Nettie's teacher (who said that Nettie was at school yesterday) and her schoolmates (who got worried when Quinn and I went to the school and asked around). I feel bad giving those children one more thing to fret about. And finally, I ask them to comfort Nettie, wherever she is. To let her know we are trying to find her.

10

The pointed toe of Miss Franny's boot wakes me up the next morning. I must have overslept, because Quinn's blanket is folded and I can hear his ax striking a log out back.

"Get up," Miss Franny says.

I rub my side where her boot jabbed between two ribs and sit up. "Sorry, I haven't slept much lately."

"And we all should suffer because of your laziness?" Miss Franny asks, going into the kitchen.

I'm not sure how my oversleeping on her front room floor is making anyone suffer, but I know Miss Franny doesn't mean for me to answer her question.

I quickly get to work on my chore list and meet Quinn by the woodpile just as he is finishing.

"I have to go to the hat shop today," I say.

"What about looking for Nettie?"

I feel awful delaying our search, but I know Ida needs me. "There's a big gala tomorrow and I can't leave Ida to finish all the orders alone. I know she accepted extra work because she thought I'd be there to help and she already gave me yesterday off."

"Ida would understand," Quinn says.

"You're right, she would understand. But her customers are the type of people who want their fancy hats finished in time to show them off at the event. If she fails them, it could really hurt her business."

Quinn raises the ax over his head and thuds it into the cold, dark earth. Then he kicks the last quarter log into his finished pile and says, "I'll go alone."

"No!" My heart jumps at his words. It never occurred to me Quinn might want to investigate on his own. "It's not safe for either of us to go alone."

"I'm not a baby, Ailis."

I know Quinn is right. He is much taller than a typical eleven-year-old and chopping wood for the boardinghouse is making his arms grow thick and strong. But big or not, eleven is still young and he is no match for an adult. "I'm just asking you to wait a few hours for me, that's all."

He lets out a ragged breath. "Fine."

"Thank you. And will you play next to the jerky cart by Ida's shop? He usually keeps his fire pit going. We can even eat lunch together."

It is a lot to ask but he says, "Okay," which makes a smile come to my face. I can't stop myself from stepping forward and giving him a hug.

"We will still look for her after you're finished," he says, not hugging me back but also not pushing me away.

"Absolutely," I say.

. . .

I only took off one day of work, so it surprises me to learn that Ida has hired another girl.

"Meet Greta," Ida says, gesturing to a dark-haired girl, who smiles at me as she stacks squares of felt. "It is just for a while."

"But I'm here today," I say.

"Finding your friend is more important. She's here to help me put the finishing touches on these orders."

On the one hand, it is thoughtful of Ida to allow me to leave and I really can't blame her for getting help. On the other hand, I don't want to take the chance of being replaced. What if this new girl is better? More helpful? Greta looks slightly younger than me but she is obviously prettier and wearing a suitable dress that I know isn't Ida's. And she isn't Irish. No doubt Lady June would find her a more appropriate choice for a shopgirl.

"I'll stay," I say.

Ida's eyes are uncertain as she says, "If you insist. That pile of felt needs to be pressed and then you can cut twelve pieces of yellow satin ribbon into ten-inch strips."

"Yes, ma'am." As I work, I keep an eye on the new girl with her raspberry smile. She is a quick study and the more she works, the more I try to show Ida how helpful I can be. I complete each task and ask for another, striving to be the better employee.

A few hours into the day, as I attempt to unravel a mess of tangled eyelet, I remember the dreadful trick I played on Lady June. Surely she will take that silly parasol to the gala tomorrow and be laughed at and then come rushing back here to demand I be fired.

And Ida is perfectly set with a replacement girl already in the shop.

I imagine Ida shaking her head and saying, *I suppose you must go.*

I can't believe I was so impulsive. What was I thinking? I pull at the eyelet in frustration.

"Achtung," Ida says in German. "Be careful, that is delicate trim."

"Sorry."

The front door pushes open, the bell tinkles, and Quinn pops his head in. "Time for lunch, Ailis?"

I rush over. "I can't take a break now," I whisper. "You go ahead and eat without me."

"Will you finish early?"

"No, I have to work a full day."

"But Nettie—"

"I can't lose this job. When we find Nettie, we'll need money to move out on our own." Then I glance in the direction of the dark-haired girl and say, "Ida hired another girl."

"Who cares? You can find a different job after we figure out what happened to Nettie."

"I care!" I say, and I am surprised at how much I really do. I push Quinn out the door.

"Fine," Quinn says. "But I'm eating lunch. Then I'm moving someplace warmer. It's cold out here, even with the fire pit."

"Where will you be?"

"I don't know," he says, clearly annoyed. Then he softens. "In the bazaar by the tea shop."

"Okay," I say, pushing him the rest of the way out and closing the door in his face.

"Is it time for your break?" Ida asks.

"I'm not hungry. Let her go on break." I gesture to Greta.

"Are you sure?"

"I'm sure." Truth be told, I am starving. I didn't eat breakfast. Still, I want to stay and work. This job may seem like a small thing to Quinn, but it is important to me. It makes me feel like a person, somehow. It gives me something to hope for in the future.

And with all I have lost, I can't bear to lose that, too.

. . .

At three o'clock, when I come upon the tea shop, I can't see Quinn and my heart starts galloping in my chest. Within a second, he comes out, eating an oversize lemon cookie.

"The owner of the tea shop gave me a cookie for my song instead of a coin," he says, holding it up and setting his fiddle down by his feet. "She said my music has been good for business."

"You scared me."

"How?"

"When I came into the bazaar, you weren't where you said you'd be."

Quinn rolls his eyes dramatically.

The sight of him eating a fresh, soft cookie makes my stomach rumble and I imagine the tang of lemon on my tongue. "Do you think she'd give you another?"

"Here," Quinn says, handing me the cookie.

"Thanks." I close my eyes and take a bite, trying to remember the last time I had a cookie. It was when Mother and Gertrude made shortbread a month or so before the fire. Mother wasn't known for her baking and, with Gertrude as a distraction, the batch came out partly burned.

Quinn and I move over to sit on a bench. "Shouldn't we finish our chores for Miss Franny?"

"Miss Franny can wait," I say.

"Fine by me," Quinn says. "Where do you think we should start?" he asks.

It's late Friday afternoon and the streets are starting to fill up. "We've already checked all the places she went," I say.

"And knocked on every door in our neighborhood," he adds.

I kick a heel in thuds against the ground. "I can only think of one person who has enough influence to help us find her."

"Who's that?"

"Mr. Olsen. Maybe he's home."

"Do you know where he lives?" Quinn asks.

"Ida might. Let's go ask her."

So we walk the two blocks back to the hat shop and ask Ida if she knows where we can find Mr. Olsen.

"Follow Canal Street over the bridge and through the rubble," she tells us. "Turn left on North Avenue and keep walking until you see a gigantic brick house on your left, with massive iron gates. A perfect waste of good money." Then she adds, mostly to herself, "Such show-offs, these Americans."

And I guess that's what she *would* think, given what she sees most days.

• • •

Quinn and I walk down Canal Street into the burned section of Chicago where we see an old man sitting inside an uprighted piano crate.

"Ailis," Quinn says under his breath.

"Just keep walking."

"But look at him."

The man's arms are bird thin, caked in dirt, and covered with open sores. His fingers bend in waves and lumps. His coat is tattered. "I see him."

"Do you think he lives in that crate?"

His blanket and a few personal items shoved into the corner clearly show he does. "Yes."

Half of Chicago is burned out, but only a small fraction of the population is gone. According to the newspaper, that forces the almost three hundred thousand remaining people to live along the surviving edges of the city. All of it makes for crowded conditions and I suppose people have to find a bed wherever they can.

Quinn goes over to the man and empties his pockets of the day's wages. I don't know how much he earned, but it looks to be a pretty good haul of coins and a few bills. The expression on the old man's face takes away any thought I have of scolding Quinn for giving up our hard-earned money. The man accepts the gift by cupping both hands above his gray, balding head and calling Quinn an angel boy. From where I stand, I think I can even see a glimmer of tears in the man's dark eyes.

Quinn returns to me and we keep walking. He doesn't say anything more until we finally make it all the way across the city to North Avenue. At this point, it is getting dark and the temperature is sliding down. "It'll be pitch-black on our way home," he says.

"We can't go back now," I say.

We turn left as Ida instructed and keep walking up the side of the street. The fire didn't go onto North Avenue and the homes in this area of the city are beautiful. The neighborhood is like a garden in the middle of a burned-out wasteland. We walk until we come upon what is unquestionably Mr. Olsen's home. It is brick and has towers and turrets and white stone walkways and an ivory bird fountain and black iron gates jabbing up into the night sky. Small lanterns line the main walkway and two enormous ones flank the front door. Ida was right; the majesty of it all seems to buzz, *Look at me, look at me, look at me.*

"Are you ready for this?" I ask Quinn.

He answers by reaching up and pulling the string that swings the call bell at the gate. It clangs out across the dimming night and then a slice of light shines between the two massive front doors. "Who's there?" the butler asks, stepping out onto the stone porch.

"Ailis and Quinn Doyle. From Peshtigo."

The light disappears as the door shuts and then the man comes back out, walking down the path. "Mr. Olsen will see you."

11

Let me do the talking," I say as the butler leads us through the grand doors and toward a library just to the left of the entry hall.

Quinn doesn't argue. He is too busy twisting his head from left to right, gawking at the magnificence that is Mr. Olsen's home.

"Mistress and Master Doyle," the butler says by way of introduction as we come into the library. I have only ever been called Ailis, not counting the list of names Miss Franny throws at me.

Mr. Olsen sits in a fat chair, leaning into a circle of lamplight and scribbling numbers in a notebook.

"Will you look at this?" Quinn says as he takes in the

shelves and shelves of books that begin down at the flowered carpet and rise all the way up to the shiny wood beams of the ceiling. Hundreds of books.

Mr. Olsen laughs and leans back in his chair. "Come," he says, "sit."

Quinn is still gawking, his chin turned up and his jaw hanging open. I take his hand and lead him over to a small couch.

"To what do I owe this visit?" Mr. Olsen asks, placing his notebook on the side table.

"We need your help," I say.

"Is something amiss at the boardinghouse?" he asks.

It is a perfect opportunity to let him know about the quality of person he hired in Miss Franny, but I know now is not the time. I can't let anything distract from why we came. "It's Nettie," I say. "She went missing two days ago."

"The little one I saw you with?" Mr. Olsen asks. "Missing, you say?"

I tell him about how Nettie disappeared and about all the places Quinn and I have searched for her.

"Have you told the police?"

"Yes," I say. "But they didn't take it seriously. Perhaps if you spoke to them?"

"Perhaps," Mr. Olsen says. "Unfortunately, children disappear all the time. It's a sad fact of our city."

"What happens to those children?" Quinn asks.

"Sold, most often—as field hands or house slaves. Sometimes they're even carried across state lines."

Quinn leans back into the cushions of the couch. "Sold."

"Has she been keeping any odd company that you know of?" Mr. Olsen asks.

"The cook from the orphanage," I say. "A man named Charlie."

Mr. Olsen drapes his arm over his chair and fiddles with his pen on the side table. Then he shakes his head. "It's not unusual for a child to seek out those she knew before being displaced."

"No," I agree, "but there is something creepy about Charlie."

I know it sounds crazy. But I also know how Charlie looked at Nettie and me when we were walking away from him and how Father Farlane said he saw Charlie at church sitting with orphans. "How do we know if she's been sold?"

"It's the most likely situation," Mr. Olsen says. "Stories of children being taken have increased dramatically since the fire. I suppose disasters of this size make people act in desperate ways."

"How will we find her?" I ask.

"Do you know her full name?"

"Nettie Cane," I say, remembering her story about how

the nuns found her on their doorstep when she was just a newborn baby. Nettie was wrapped in a loosely crocheted brown blanket and tucked into a basket made from sugarcane reeds. The nuns told her they named her Nettie after the blanket that reminded them of a fishing net and gave her the surname Cane to honor the basket in which she was delivered, as well as her sweet nature. It was one of Nettie's favorite stories.

"That will help some," Mr. Olsen says. "I'll put a few feelers out and be in touch if I hear anything. I'm sorry there is not more I can offer."

"Thank you," I say.

Mr. Olsen stands up. "In the meantime, remember you are both children yourselves. Be careful who you question and where you search. You don't want to end up in the same situation."

"I'd never let that happen," Quinn says.

"These people are not to be trifled with," Mr. Olsen says. "A child is nothing against their type of evil. Promise me you'll be careful."

I can see Quinn is bothered by being called a child twice in a row but he nods as Mr. Olsen walks us to the back door, where a work wagon is parked. "My driver will return you to the boardinghouse. You shouldn't be walking the streets at night." We thank Mr. Olsen once more and climb up on the front bench of a simple buckboard.

The driver is a quiet man and we are left alone with our thoughts. The moon, heavy and low, pours silver light out across Chicago's empty streets. All those people crowding the sidewalks on our way to Mr. Olsen's have disappeared. The only sound is the wheels crunching against dirty snow and the steady clopping of the horse's hooves.

I lean in to Quinn and whisper, "I can't stop thinking about what Mr. Olsen said."

Quinn just nods.

I look at the piles of rubble and empty lots where buildings have been demolished. Here in the dark it seems as if anyone could be lurking behind the half-tumbled walls.

We ride in silence the rest of the way back to the boardinghouse. When we arrive, Miss Franny is angry we missed our chores and has a list waiting for us to start first thing in the morning.

After we settle down for bed, Quinn says, "That was some house. We could live there without him even noticing."

"The servants would notice," I say.

"They would just think we were other servants. New servants. Did you see all those books?"

I think Quinn would have been quite a scholar had our cranberry farm allowed him the opportunity. "I saw them," I say.

Quinn rolls over and quickly falls asleep.

I close my eyes, but sleep seems far away. Instead, images

of Nettie keep coming to mind. Scenes of her being dragged off by some brutish thug and sold into slavery. Mental pictures of her asking about when she can return to school or see Quinn and me again—and being told, *Never*.

I can't stand how those thoughts make me feel so I get up, light a small lamp, and begin washing dinner dishes. I work through the night—scrubbing the grime on the wall behind the stove, wiping down the pantry shelves, and quietly humming an Irish tune. It is one I remember Mother humming while we milked the cows. It is winsome and happy and helps keep my mind clear.

Before morning light even has a chance to slide through the cracks of the house, I pull back the curtains in the front room and look out the window to the trees along the side of the yard.

"What'd ya go and do that for?" Quinn groans.

"It's morning."

"Barely. The rooster hasn't even crowed yet and Miss Franny's not awake."

I cinch the tie on the curtain as Miss Franny's voice comes down the hallway. "I'm always awake." She stops in the doorway. "Get your lazy-rat bones off my floor already."

I don't know if it is the lack of sleep or the stress of everything that is happening—or perhaps both—but seeing Miss

Franny makes my blood boil in my veins and, even though I know it is not true, I find myself blurting out the meanest thing I can think of. "Did you sell Nettie?"

Quinn is picking up his blanket and freezes mid-fold.

Miss Franny puts her fists on her hips. "That girl is dim-witted and sickly. How could I sell something so pathetic, even if I wanted to? Who would pay?" The anger is making a muscle under her right eye twitch. "If you want someone to blame, you should take a good look in the mirror."

"How is it my fault?"

"Do you think I am a fool? I know you are not really attending school. When I went by to ask about Nettie, the teacher had no idea who you were. Maybe if you weren't such a selfish liar, you would have watched over her."

She is still standing halfway across the room, but it is like she reached out and punched me in the gut. I keep my voice low and strong. "Things like flowers and trees and smoke make Nettie's nose runny, but you know she's not dim-witted."

Miss Franny inspects her fingernails casually, trying to look calm. "Blame me all you want, but we both know you are the one responsible. Whatever happens to that girl is on your head." She quits looking at her hand and shoots me a glare. "So much for the perfect Ailis Doyle."

Sam comes up behind her and wraps his arms around her waist. "Aw, ease up on the kid, Fran."

She pushes him off and flits her eyes over to Quinn and me. "I don't really care what you liars do as long as you finish your work here first."

I take off through the kitchen, out the back door, and sit down on the last step.

Quinn comes out after me and says, "You know Miss Franny is wrong. What happened to Nettie isn't your fault."

I'm not convinced. "I just don't know how Sam can stand her."

"Maybe it's all the ale he drinks."

I smile and look out of the corner of my eye at Quinn. "At least it sounds as if she's going to leave us alone a bit."

"As long as we keep waking up at five in the morning to do her work."

"True," I say.

"Let's get walking," he says, reaching down to take my hand and help me up.

"Will you play by Ida's today?" I ask.

"No. Her shop isn't busy enough for me and the butcher shop is played out. It's time for a new corner."

I want Quinn to play where I can watch over him, but I know he has his own mind. So we head into the city and find a busy corner where three pushcarts are clustered around a blazing fire pit. One vendor is selling strips of dried and salted pig fat, another is selling hot coffee, and the last is selling trinkets and velvet bags. It is an unusual assortment but the street is busy and it seems a safe enough place to leave Quinn.

"Be careful," I say, expecting him to roll his eyes or tell me he isn't a baby.

But he doesn't. He just dips his chin in agreement and says, "You too."

I watch him find an open spot close to the fire and set his fiddle case down. He unlatches one lock and is starting to unlatch the other when a man comes up to him and says something, waving a hand wildly. I notice he holds a mouth harp in the other hand. It is a teardrop-shaped instrument that you pluck against your mouth.

Quinn relocks his fiddle case and comes over to me.

"What'd he say?" I ask.

"He told me to scram. He said it was his corner and that I was trying to steal a piece of his action."

"What action?"

"Exactly," Quinn says.

"Come to Ida's with me."

"Forget it," Quinn says. "I'm not going to let this guy win. I'm going to stand right next to him and show him how it's really done."

"You don't know anything about that guy," I say. "He could be dangerous."

"He's a lousy drunk with a mouth harp. And he's half my weight. I could knock him out cold if I had to."

It's true. The man is grown, but he is short and scrawny. "Some fights aren't worth having."

"I'll let my music do the fighting for me."

I have a minute before Ida is expecting me so I stay on the street by Quinn and watch him play.

It is an interesting duel of sorts. Quinn plays his best music, twisting and bouncing to the tunes like Father often did. In response, the drunk plucks twangy songs out on his mouth harp. They stare each other down, but they are polite and each waits for the other's song to finish before taking his next turn.

As they play back and forth, a crowd begins to gather. Brick masons and shopkeepers and mothers and men in dark suits all bundled in coats and scarves. The people cheer and turn from one side of the street to the other with each song.

People drop some money into the man's hat but the coins fall like raindrops into Quinn's fiddle case.

After four rounds of songs, the man picks up his hat, nods at Quinn as if to say, *you win*, and goes into the pub three doors down. That causes the crowd to cheer even louder and toss another round of coins at Quinn's feet.

When everyone disperses, Quinn gathers the money and asks, "Who's the fool now?"

"I've got to go to work," I say, ignoring his question.

"I'll come with you. I've made enough money for now."

"Thanks."

As we start walking, we hear the tolling of bells and stop on a corner as a funeral procession comes down the street. A wagon carries a small pine coffin. Clearly, it is a child being taken to the cemetery. The horses pulling the wagon are draped in heavy black fabric with gold tassels hanging from the corners. The women wear crepe veils of black and the men wear black suits. A boy, about ten years old, walks behind the procession carrying a large black feather on a golden stick. One man on each side swings a brass bell, warding off evil and warning traffic of the coming procession.

Traffic parts and pedestrians move to the sidewalk.

I look over to Quinn, whose face is the same flat gray color as the sky.

When the procession finally passes and is down the road a good distance, he turns to me. "We need to find her, Ailis. We need to find her soon."

I am entirely without words so I just follow Quinn over to Ida's shop. It feels wrong going into work after watching that funeral procession, but I have to do it. It's not that Ida doesn't want us to look for Nettie—she would understand. But there is nowhere new to look and nothing else to do but wait to hear from Mr. Olsen.

"Any news?" Ida asks as we come through the door.

I shake my head.

"Aye, do not worry, *Liebling*, angels will surely watch over one so small."

"What's a *Liebling*?" Quinn asks.

"It's a term of endearment. It's German," Greta says from her spot behind the counter.

Quinn smiles at the girl and I am annoyed. "Quinn offered to help today," I say to Ida, "since we're so busy with holiday orders." Maybe the new girl is pretty *and* German, but Quinn and I can outwork anyone.

"I'll not trust those big hands with a needle," Ida says, "but it would be nice if the windows could be washed. There is still so much soot and grime that gets kicked up into the air."

"Where can I find a bucket?" Quinn asks.

"In the storeroom, and there is a pump for water as well."

Quinn goes to get the water and I sit down to finish sewing lavender ribbon on a pair of white gloves.

"Do you ever think of going home?" Ida asks me, her hands busy cutting felt.

"I don't have a home."

"Did your parents not own your farm?"

I am surprised. "You mean go back to Peshtigo? There's nothing left."

"There is land, yes? Earth to till and a flat spot to rebuild a small cottage. Maybe there is even a place for a row of carrots or patch of peas?"

The lavender ribbon bunches up on my thread, causing a ripple in the trim. I start unpicking my stitches to smooth it out. "I don't know," I say. "It's too hard to think about now. Do you ever consider going back to Germany?"

Ida sighs. "All the time. But it is too late for an old woman like me."

Greta joins in. "Do you remember spring in Deutschland, Ida? The festivals?"

"Aye, how could I not?"

Greta starts talking in German and takes Ida's attention. I don't know what they are saying but whatever it is, it makes the delicate lines around Ida's blue eyes bunch up into a smile.

It is good to see her happy, but I can't help feeling a touch of jealousy at how well they seem to get along. At what they have in common.

"I suppose spring is beautiful wherever you live," I say, trying to join their conversation.

"Perhaps," Ida says. "But nothing compares to spring in your homeland. Those memories are just a little brighter, just a little warmer than any others."

Greta smiles and I feel excluded again. Why should I even care? "Oh, no!" I say as the lavender ribbon knots up.

Ida puts her work down and comes over to me. "You should go look for your friend," she says. "Your mind is not on the work and I don't blame you."

"There's nowhere else to look."

"Can the police help?"

"They told us not to get our hopes up."

"The police," Ida says, going over to her table. "*Dummkopf!* These police, what do they know about anything?"

"Mr. Olsen thinks she has been sold."

Ida stills her needle in the air. "I have heard of such things happening."

I hang my head and let the tears slide down my cheeks, making wet splotches on the ribbon in my hands.

Quinn comes in from the storeroom, holding a bucket of water in one hand and rags in the other. "What happened?" he asks when he sees me.

Ida hurries over to my side and begins patting my shoulder. "Do not cry."

"It's all right," Quinn says. "It helps."

I look at my brother through my tears and wonder how he knows that. "I'm afraid I have ruined these gloves," I say to Ida.

"They will dry. No one will be able to tell." Then she claps her hands. "I think it is time for *Schokoladentorte*."

"Chocolate cake?" I ask, remembering the word.

"I have some upstairs. All of us, we will go."

"What about the customers who are coming to pick up their goods?"

"I'll put a sign in the window for them to knock," Ida says, walking over to my side. "I know you are worried about your friend, but if she truly has been sold then she is still alive, yes? And sleeping under a roof and eating something each day? Mr. Olsen is a powerful man. He will help you find her." Then her dusty blue eyes get all soft. "There is a saying I remember from when I was a girl, *Liebe ist wie Wasser*. It means, Love is like water. You see, when love hits a wall, it doesn't stop. It just bends around the wall and keeps flowing. Your friend Nettie knows she is loved and that will carry her through this terrible time." Then she tugs on her apron. "We Germans drink ale or eat cake at times of happiness and also at times of sadness. You are too young for ale, so you must have cake."

Ida locks the door, puts a sign in the window, and then leads me and Greta up the stairs to her apartment. Quinn offers to stay and wash the windows but Ida tells him it would be rude not to eat with the rest of us. That makes Quinn smile and put down his cloth and tell her he would hate to offend her by turning down cake. Maybe, he says, he should even eat extra to show proper respect.

When we get to Ida's apartment above the shop, she pulls

down five china plates and slices five pieces of cake. One for herself, one for Greta, an oversize piece for Quinn, one for me, and then one for Nettie. When I ask her about the last slice, Ida says, "We will live as if she could walk through our door at any minute and, someday soon, it will happen."

Miss Franny slaps her ankle as I finish wiping down the breakfast table Monday morning and says, "I think that was a flea."

"You don't have house pets. Everyone knows fleas can't live without a host animal, especially in December."

"That is true, and you are a lazy rat. A rat who brings fleas into my house." She pinches another nonexistent flea from her skirt and says, "You probably picked them up from that O'Leary family."

I think of Mrs. O'Leary. I stopped by to check on her, but she wouldn't come to the door. "Mrs. O'Leary has locked herself up in her house and won't even come outside anymore," I say. "I haven't seen her in weeks."

"A woman that filthy doesn't have to come out of her house to give you fleas. Just walking on her side of the road is enough."

It is a horrible thing to say and Miss Franny knows it. Catherine and Patrick O'Leary were completely exonerated from any charges related to Chicago's fire. The commission found no evidence they were in the barn and said the fire could have been started by any number of things, including a stray spark from a chimney or a passerby with a pipe.

Miss Franny is aware of the facts but, along with most of Chicago, wants to keep believing that the O'Learys are guilty.

"Is there anything more I can do before I leave?" I ask, ignoring her comment.

"Are the chickens fed?"

"Yes."

"And their coop cleaned?"

"I cleaned it yesterday."

She thinks a bit. "What about the kitchen and dishes?"

"Finished."

"Ironing?"

"Folded and put on the hall table."

"Fine, go. But watch where you walk and what you pick up along the way. Fleas were not part of the deal when you were given a room."

"Quinn and I don't have a room. You make us sleep on the floor." The yellow-toothed boarder is gone and another hasn't come, but she still makes us sleep on the front rug.

She slaps at her ankle again. "Which is why my floor is now covered with bloodsucking fleas."

Two women boarders start down the stairs. Miss Franny stands up tall and whispers, "Go on before you scare away my paying customers with that cabbage face of yours."

"I'm leaving," I say, taking my coat from the nail by the back door and going outside to meet Quinn.

Sam is helping him chop the wood.

"Why do you love Miss Franny?" I ask him.

He stops chopping. "Who said anything about love?"

"I saw you put your arms around her."

"Fran and I have a sort of symbiotic relationship. We lean on each other because we have no one else."

"You have me and Quinn."

"Not exactly what I mean, but thanks all the same." He swings his ax down into another log. "Even the hardest woman has a soft side. It just takes the right man to find it."

"Any word on Nettie yet?" I ask him, wanting to change the subject. Sam has been asking around at various pubs, listening to the news that slides along the underbelly of the city.

"Not yet, but I'm keeping my ear to the ground."

"It'd be nice if we could bring her home before Christmas," Quinn says. "It's next Monday, you know. Just one week from today."

Sam moves his ax up to his shoulder. "Ah, joyous Noel." There is definite sarcasm in his words.

I can't imagine having Christmas without Mother, Father, and Gertrude. And knowing Nettie will be gone makes it worse. "This coming Monday will be like any other day," I say. "We have nothing to celebrate."

"You can't ignore Christmas," Quinn says. "Do you think Miss Franny will let us light a candle in the window on Christmas Eve?"

It is an Irish tradition to have the youngest child light a candle and place it in the front room window on Christmas Eve. Mother was the youngest in her family and spoke fondly of her memories of being the candle girl when she was growing up. Gertrude only got to light the candle one year—she was too young before that.

"Of course, it *should* be Nettie who lights it, since she's the youngest," Quinn says, his voice falling back down into a sad, low place as he remembers how the tradition works.

"You can light it for her," Sam says. "Just this year."

"Miss Franny's not going to let us decorate her house or have any part in her holiday," I say.

"I might be able to convince her otherwise," Sam says.

"Don't bother." I'm not about to celebrate anything—much less Christmas—with the likes of Miss Franny. "Let's go," I say to Quinn. "I can't be late for work."

I don't need Quinn to tell me Christmas is coming. I see it in every moment of every day. It is a circle of holly on someone's door and a simple red ribbon on a lamppost. It is a song drifting out from behind church windows and the clean scent of a rare pine tree still left on the edge of the city. It is white snowflakes falling out of a mostly blue sky. It is children laughing.

No matter how I've tried, I can't escape it.

• • •

"You will come next Monday, yes?" Ida asks for the fourth time.

"I don't know."

"You will come. And Quinn will come. And we will set a place at our table for Nettie."

"What about Greta?" I ask.

"She has family to spend the holiday with. I have given her a week off and, because business has been so good, I've asked her to come back again after the New Year."

I keep sweeping the shop floor.

"It would be unkind to leave an old woman alone on Christmas," she says. "You must do me this one favor. I ask so little."

I sweep the pile of dirt into a corner. "Okay," I say. And then, because I know she is just trying to help, "Thank you." I don't want to celebrate Christmas, but being with Ida will be better than staying at the boardinghouse.

"Good!" Ida claps her hands.

I'm leaning over, sweeping my pile of dirt onto a dustpan, when the bell above the door chimes.

"Hello, Ida."

I immediately recognize the voice as Lady June's and stay hunched over in the corner, wishing I could disappear into the woodwork.

"Good morning," Ida says. "Don't you look lovely in your purple cloak. And that brooch, oh my! I have never seen anything so fine."

"It once belonged to the Duchess of Yorkshire," Lady June says, referring to the brooch. "It's a royal jewel."

"Then it is befitting for you to wear it," Ida goes on.

I can't see how Lady June responds, but I imagine her chins quivering and her head nodding in agreement.

And then Ida asks *the* question. The one I was dreading but knew was coming. "How was the benefit gala?"

I try to shrink down farther into the corner.

"That is what I came to speak to you about," Lady June says.

"Tell me," Ida says.

I feel a flush across my cheeks.

"You in the corner," Lady June says, "come over here."

I stand up and turn around. Secretly, I have allowed myself to dream of apprenticing under Ida and being able to open a millinery shop of my own someday. But those ambitions now feel like a delicate spiderweb this clodhopping woman is about to tromp through and destroy. She is going to expose me for the mean-spirited girl I am. What choice will Ida have but to fire me? Perhaps Miss Franny has been right about me all along.

"Yes, ma'am?" I say, trying to hold my voice steady.

"You are the one responsible." Lady June is pointing her sausage finger at my face. "It is because of you that everyone was staring at me."

I drop my head and begin to apologize but she surprises me by slapping her hands down onto her skirt and saying, "It was a dilly of an afternoon! Even the mayor was craning his neck to get a look at my parasol as I walked into the event. I was the talk of the city!" Then she turns her attention to Ida. "Truth be told, I don't believe you should hire her kind to deal with money and customers. The Irish are known thieves and best at menial labor, behind the scenes. That is why my husband uses them in the sewers for his business. However, this is an exception to that rule." Her finger is wagging in my face again. "Despite the blood running through this peasant's veins, she has been able to learn under your diligent tutelage. Well done, Ida Muench."

I can't believe my luck! Lady June is so stuck on herself she mistook people's shock for adoration.

"It's not fair to say the Irish—" Ida begins, but I jump over to her side.

"Thank you, Lady June. You are most kind." I give a small curtsy. "We are blessed to be in your service."

Lady June smiles, causing her chins to jiggle some more. "Yes," she says, "you are."

She turns and walks out the door.

"That woman," Ida says, shaking her head. "I have known her for years. She comes off as high society but the truth is she grew up middle class and married into money. Not even old money, either. Her husband runs Chicago's biggest rat extermination company. Absolute Exterminators. That's the business she was referring to."

"She gets all her money from killing rats?"

"Of course she doesn't do the work herself." Ida goes back to her table. "Her husband has a large crew and I hear business has been good since the fire."

"Wow, all that money from rats."

Ida begins threading a needle. "My Gunther always said a job is a job. Honest work shouldn't be judged, but I do believe Lady June overcompensates for a few things. No matter how she tries, she'll never fit in with the upper crust of Chicago. She knows it and all those snobs she associates with know it, too. It's not enough to have wealth. High-society people believe it must come from the right source. The truth about Lady June is, a million dollars of rat money will—in the end—still be rat money."

14

Quinn and I go to Christmas Eve Mass at Father Farlane's church. We aren't looking for spiritual guidance. We are looking for Charlie. So I change into one of Ida's dresses that I have started keeping in the shed and walk to church with the rest of the Irish quarter. Christmas Eve and Easter are the two holidays when almost all of us Catholics attend Mass, so the church is packed to the rafters.

"I don't see him," I whisper to Quinn as we find seats in a pew near the rear of the building.

"We just got here," Quinn says. "Be patient."

It is cold outside, but the building is warm from so many people crowding in together. I take off my coat and stretch my neck up, looking across the crowd for a bald head. There are several of them, but none belong to Charlie.

Father Farlane's voice rings out from the altar, filling the room with echoes of chants and song. As a group, we stand and sit and then we kneel and stand again. I glance over to Quinn. "Are you looking for him?" I ask.

He gives me a *shush* look, like I am being irreverent, and then speaks in unison with the crowd.

I am on my own.

"Wait here," I say, ducking down past Quinn and into the side aisle. I stand with my back against the high stone wall of the church and inch down the walkway as I scan each row of parishioners.

At one point I pass by a boy about four years old who is the last person in the row, standing next to someone who must be his mother. She is busy participating in the Mass, but he waves to get my attention and then points up to the ceiling where a brown bird is flying in circles high above our heads.

I keep my hand next to my body but point a finger up, letting him know I see the bird, too. Then I smile, wave good-bye, and move on down the rows, back on the hunt for bald heads.

When I finally work my way up to the front, I see Charlie. He is standing in the middle of a row of children who are wearing mostly tattered clothing. I have no doubt they are displaced orphans.

His signature toothpick is sticking out of the corner of his mouth. Who chews a toothpick in church?

Charlie turns and stares straight at me with an awful smile. He twirls his toothpick and winks.

I run—flat-out run—up the aisle to where Quinn is sitting.

"What are you doing?" he whispers. "You shouldn't be running in church."

I saw Charlie, I mouth, sliding in next to him.

Quinn stands on his tiptoes and looks down to the front. "I don't see him."

"Trust me, he's there. He's with a bunch of orphans, too. Probably picking them off one by one."

The lady behind us leans forward and tells us to hush. I apologize and Quinn lowers his voice again. "I want to talk to him afterward. I have an idea."

"What kind of idea?"

"You'll see."

Quinn goes back to following the service, but I can't concentrate on a single thing. I sit on the bench and double over, resting my head against my knees. The thought of Nettie being in the hands of a louse like Charlie makes the acid in my stomach roll up into my throat. I try to breathe slowly and fight to keep from vomiting all over Father Farlane's floor.

• • •

When the last hymn is over and people have begun filing out the doors I say, "Maybe we should talk to the other orphans."

"You go ahead," Quinn says. "I want to speak with Charlie before he leaves. I should do it alone."

"No way."

"Charlie knows who you are. He'll be more careful with what he says. I'm going to ask him if he knows of any work. I'll say I lost my family in the fire and that someone on the street said he might be able to help me."

"He's dangerous," I say, my whisper sharp and direct. "I should stay with you."

"If he's innocent, he'll say he can't help me. But if he's taking children, he'll be very interested in my problem. If you're there, standing at my side, he won't fall for the bait." Quinn stands up. "I'm going to wait by the main doors. Everyone seems to be going out that way."

I really want to talk to the other children, but am more concerned about leaving Quinn alone with Charlie. I push through the crowd behind my brother. "I'm not leaving you."

He sighs. "At least hide behind those curtains."

I look over to the red velvet fabric flanking a large stained-glass window depicting a tree in the Garden of Eden.

"Hurry," Quinn says.

"Promise me you'll stay here and not go out the door with him," I say.

"I can handle myself."

I catch Quinn's gaze and give him the most serious look I can manage. Then I step behind the curtain.

Nearly everyone leaves before Charlie comes down the aisle. He is talking to a little girl with blond curls, but a woman steps into the doorway and calls her name.

"Bye, Charlie," the girl says, leaving with the woman.

"So, you're Charlie? From the orphanage?" Quinn asks, coming out to meet him in the aisle.

I stay behind the curtain, watching through a slit in the fabric.

I can barely hear what they are saying. Quinn asks about work. Charlie moves his toothpick from one side of his mouth to the other and I hear him say something about earning more money than Quinn can imagine. And also something about being part of a new family.

At one point, Charlie tries to put his arm around Quinn, but my brother is smart enough to step back. "Let me think about it," I hear Quinn say. "I'll let you know next Sunday."

Charlie shifts awkwardly and then smiles his slimy grin. "Sure, kid," he says. Father Farlane comes up behind Quinn, which makes Charlie leave.

"Any word on your friend?" Father Farlane asks Quinn.

"Not yet."

I slide out from the curtain.

"Well," Father Farlane says, "I'm keeping her in my prayers."

Quinn thanks him and when we are sure Charlie is long gone we walk out and stand at the side of the church. I button my coat. At some point, I had put the yellow chalk in my coat pocket so I pull it out and draw a flower on the stone wall of the building.

"Should you be doing that?" Quinn asks.

I ignore him. "What'd Charlie say?"

"He said the work wasn't fancy but if you aren't afraid of dark, tight places, then you can make a living."

"Doing what?"

Quinn takes the chalk out of my hand and says, "Catching rats."

• • •

The next day is Christmas and we are at Ida's. When I tell her that we saw Charlie, she says, "Do not worry so much, *Liebling.*"

Quinn says, "It's not fair for you to ruin everyone's Christmas."

Still, I can't put my worries about Nettie aside. "Charlie said there is work killing rats," I tell Ida as she cuts into a fruitcake. "He even offered Quinn a job."

"That doesn't seem right," Ida says. "What good would a child be against an army of rats?"

I chew on my bottom lip and think about Lady June and her husband's business.

Ida puts a piece of fruitcake, which she calls *Stollen*, in front of me and pours milk into my glass. Then she serves Quinn the same thing and sits down. "I know you are worried about your friend," she says. "And with good cause. But you need to look at the matter in a different light. For Nettie's sake, you must choose to be positive. Let me tell you a story."

I'm not in the mood for a story so I begin picking the dried cherries and raisins out of my cake and placing them along the strip of gold that rims my plate.

"I came to America as a young bride," Ida begins. "Barely twenty years old with nothing but a few coins and a husband who loved me. It was enough.

"The only English words I knew were *apple* and *cat*. Can you believe it? I'm not even sure where I learned those two words. Oh, what a mess I was in." She laughs to herself. "But then Gunther found a woman who offered English lessons. We didn't have money to pay her so he told her I would make her a bonnet—the most beautiful bonnet she would ever own—if only she would be our teacher. Lucky for us, she said yes."

Once all the fruit is picked out of the cake, I start with the nuts. I am slowly shredding Ida's hard work but she ignores it and keeps telling her story.

"Learning English came easy for Gunther, but was very hard for me," Ida says. "I'm still learning it, really. At the beginning, it felt impossible. The words are so different from my beautiful German language. And the verbs! Those were the most difficult of all."

I pop a dried cherry in my mouth and chew slowly.

"My teacher worked hard to help me understand the verbs—*to walk, to eat, to dance, to speak. He walks, I walk, we are walking* . . . it was all so challenging."

I look over at Quinn, who is on the edge of his seat, lost in Ida's story, and I wonder what any of this has to do with Nettie.

"But do you know what the most important verb in the English language is?"

I eat another cherry and, when I realize she has stopped talking and is looking at me with wide, expectant eyes, say, "Are you asking me?"

"Of course I am asking you."

"Not really."

"It is the verb *to be. I am, you are, she is* . . . Can you think of anything more important than those words?"

I swallow the cherry, thinking.

She goes on. *"I am Ida. You are Ailis. She is Nettie. This is Quinn."* She touches his shoulder. "There is great power in those words. How else can we use the *to be* verb? Let's try *I am happy, you are strong, she is going to be found."*

I fidget with a walnut on my plate, looking down.

"Now you try," Ida says, lifting my chin to meet her gaze. "You show me how you understand the power of that verb."

Water rims my eyes and I blink quickly, trying to push back the tears.

Ida sits patiently.

Finally, I say, *"I am Ailis, you are Ida, she is Nettie."*

"What else?" Ida whispers.

I swallow again. *"I am a survivor, you are my friend, she is brave."*

"Yes," Ida says softly. Then she looks to Quinn. "Your turn."

Quinn nods. *"I am Quinn, you are Ida, and she is Ailis."* He tilts his head in my direction when he says my name and I am surprised he pulled me into his *to be* list.

"And?" Ida says.

Quinn goes on. *"I am strong, you are old, and she is a better-than-average sister."*

"Humph," Ida says. "Old?"

The side of Quinn's mouth twitches up into a half smile.

"Fine," Ida says. *"You are strong, Ailis is a wonderful sister, and I am an old woman.*" She turns to me. "Isn't it interesting how a single verb can change your vision? Choose to conjugate your life with positivity." Ida stands up and goes over to her stove. "We only have one Christmas each year and I have spent the last eight of them by myself. This year I am blessed to have company at my table. I do not want to let it pass without celebration."

And so we don't.

There are no Christmas trees to be found in the city but we string lace around the kitchen. Quinn teaches Ida the lyrics to an Irish holiday tune. She in turn teaches us that *Tannenbaum* means Christmas tree in German and all about how the first traditional Christmas tree was set up in Freiburg, Germany, in 1419 by the town bakers. As she tells it, they decorated the tree with fruit, nuts, and baked goods and set it outside of their shop. Then, when the holiday was over, they invited all the children in town to come together and eat the treats hidden in the tree's branches.

She seems so proud of that story.

We eat roasted goose with apple stuffing, red cabbage, and Ida's potato dumplings, which are delicious. After dinner is finished and the dishes are washed, Quinn says, "Time for presents," and walks to the corner of the room where his fiddle is propped against a table. "It's not much but . . ."

"It's perfect," Ida says, not even knowing what he has planned. She pulls me over to sit on her couch. "Play for us."

Quinn tunes his strings—which always sounds like a screeching bird—and tucks his fiddle under his chin. "You may not know this song, Ida, but Ailis does. It was one of our father's favorites."

Then he begins playing "Johnny, I Hardly Knew Ye." It's a jaunty marching song but the lyrics are terribly tragic—all about a soldier who comes back from war unrecognizable. Luckily, Quinn doesn't sing the lyrics.

When he finishes, Ida bounces up out of her seat, clapping.

I give my brother a hug. "Thank you," I whisper in his ear as I pull away.

"I feel like they are here with us," Quinn says, putting his fiddle into the case.

"Of course they are," Ida says. "They are with you always. Some evenings, when the house is too quiet, I talk out loud to my Gunther. I tell him about the work and the crazy people who have come into the shop and all about the spunky Irish girl who helps me keep our business going." She reaches for two boxes on the floor next to her couch. "My turn for presents. One for you," she says, handing a box to Quinn, "and one for you," she says, handing the other to me.

"You shouldn't have," I say. "I don't have anything for you."

"An old woman such as myself has no need for more trinkets. You are young with so much life ahead of you. Take this and be happy."

Quinn opens his box and pulls out a soot-gray bowler.

"A young man deserves a proper hat," Ida says.

"I love it!" Quinn puts it on and walks around the room with his hands on his hips and his chest puffed out. I have to admit he looks good.

"Now you," Ida says to me.

I open my box and pull out a bonnet made of crushed blue velvet and white lace. "Isn't this the hat you were making for the mayor's wife?"

"So I told a lie, shoot me. Put it on, put it on."

I go over to the window, using the dark pane as a looking glass, and slide the hat over my wavy hair.

Ida comes up behind me, putting her hands on my shoulders. I can see the reflection of her face in the window glass just slightly behind mine. "I will add a bit more to my *to be* verb list," she says. *"I am amazed, you are beautiful."*

15

Nettie has been gone for two weeks when Quinn and I find ourselves standing next to the buckeye tree, waiting for Sam. Earlier, he took Miss Franny by the hand, flashed a smile, and asked if Quinn and I could leave our chores to attend tonight's celebration with him. Several businesses in Chicago are coming together to commemorate the rebuilding with a huge bonfire, which seems an ironic choice to me. Miss Franny wasn't happy about his request and didn't want to join us but she can't say no to Sam.

"He said he'd take care of a few things and then would try to meet us here," Quinn says, which probably means Sam stopped by the pub. "But he also said we could go over without him if he was running late."

Icy wind swirls and cuts through the seams in my coat. My feet ache from standing on the frozen ground. The sun is fading behind dark clouds. Night is coming again.

"I'm freezing and I bet he's already over there," I say, wrapping my arms across my middle.

"Let's go then," Quinn says.

We head over to the open field where swarms of people are already gathering.

"Look at that!" Quinn says, pointing to a pile of wood at least fifteen feet high.

"I hope they have firemen around. And water."

"It'll be all right."

We push our way through the mob to the front. Someone bumps into me from behind and I grab on to Quinn's arm.

"Stay close," I say.

He hears me but takes off anyway, saying, "There's Sam."

Everyone looks the same to me—men and women in dark coats and hats, scarves wrapped up around their chins. Children clinging to their parents' coat pockets or sleeves.

"Wait!" I copy the children and grab Quinn's coat, being pulled along as he zigzags through the masses, over to the other side of the wood piled up for the bonfire.

"Hiya, Sam," Quinn says when we meet up.

"Hiya back," Sam says, grinning wide and smacking Quinn on the shoulder.

"We waited for you at the tree," I say, aggravated.

"But you found me after all, didn't you?" Sam says. Then he turns to Quinn. "Where's your fiddle?"

"I left it at the boardinghouse."

"Too bad," Sam says. "Crowds this big can be a real payday for a kid with talent like yours."

"I don't want to work tonight."

Just then, some guy walks up to a podium that is built onto a mini-stage next to the woodpile. His collar is winter white, starched heavily and pushing up his sagging neck. "People! People!" he shouts into the crowd. After a minute, the group quiets down and listens. "We are coming together as a city, like a phoenix rising from the ashes. As our great Mayor Medill says, this new Chicago will be mightier than ever before!"

The crowd goes wild.

"All right, all right, people!" the man shouts, lifting his arms up high and then lowering them slowly, like he is pushing down the volume. "It is time to start our celebration."

A loudmouth from the crowd yells out, "Then go get Mrs. O'Leary and her cow. They're good at lighting fires!"

The crowd laughs and pushes one another and murmurs about the reckless Mrs. O'Leary and her awful cow.

"Idiots," I say, but mostly to myself because I know I am outnumbered.

Somewhere around the edges of the woodpile, lines of fire climb up and, within seconds, a bonfire is raging.

"To our Chicago!" the man at the podium shouts, again throwing both arms up high over his head.

People cheer, breaking into dance as musicians begin to play. Sam swings his arm into mine and twirls around in a dance, his eyes shining from the firelight. Then he takes Quinn's hand and begins threading through the crowd, knees high and head moving from side to side. It is a dance of joy and unity.

"*Let go*, Ailis," Sam says when he wraps back around and sees me standing still. "Just let go and dance!"

And, despite myself, I take his hand, lift my knees, and dance with the rest of Chicago. I flap my arms out like a bird, and jump little sprite jumps. I give myself completely to the celebration.

Sam, Quinn, and I dance for over two hours, until the bonfire dwindles to a mass of embers and the firemen step in to wet everything down.

"Let's go over there," Sam says, pointing to a row of rocks along the side of a building.

We sit a minute to catch our breath and watch as everyone separates into their own lives once again.

"That was fun," Quinn says through broken breaths.

Sam nods.

I pull my coat tighter. The sweat along my back makes me cold now that I have stopped dancing. "Maybe we should go."

"In a minute," Sam says. "I heard about a rat exterminating company today that uses children to do some of the work. It's called Absolute Exterminators and is owned by a guy named Rold Blume."

That makes Lady June's name June Blume. "Do they have Nettie?"

"I don't know for certain, but word has it they've got some brute filching children off the streets."

"Charlie," I say, guessing.

"Ronnie at the pub told me this creep's getting twenty bucks a head. He even said the guy would give me a cut if I came up with a kid or two." He must see my expression because he quickly adds, "Don't worry, I'm not interested in that kind of dough."

"Twenty dollars is nothing for a person's life."

"It's enough for this guy."

"Yeah," Quinn says, "because it's not *his* life he's selling off."

Sam picks up a pebble and tosses it across the road. "He's a chump."

"What can we do?" I ask.

Sam cranes his neck, looking across the road to the

bonfire area. "Ronnie thinks the company is bunking these kids in a burned-out five-story over on Monroe Street. If they're working tonight, we might get lucky and see something."

We head over to the building on Monroe Street, which used to be a grand hotel called the Monroe. Now it's charred brick walls with squares of tin blocking the window openings.

"People live there?" Quinn asks.

"People live wherever they can nowadays," Sam says.

I think of the man Quinn and I saw living in the piano crate.

Sam points at three shadows slinking out from around the corner of the building. I start to go over but Sam puts his hand on my shoulder. "Hold on," he whispers. An older boy comes out behind those three shadows and begins trailing them. "The overseer."

"How are we gonna ask those kids about Nettie if they're being watched?" I say.

Sam crosses his arms and rocks back on his heels. "That's a good question."

"And I don't get why they're even taking children in the first place," I add. "There are so many people out of work right now, why don't they hire adults?"

"Free labor is better than paid labor any day of the week,"

Sam says. "Plus, children are small and can go into areas a grown man can't."

"What kind of areas?" I ask.

"Rickety top floors of burned buildings. Skinny sewer pipes. Chimneys—just about anywhere a rat likes to hide."

Thinking of Nettie in places like that makes me queasy.

"Do you really think she could be in that building?" Quinn asks.

"Hard to say for sure," Sam says. "The truth is, we don't know if Charlie took Nettie."

"I bet he did," I say.

"There's no real evidence of it," Sam says. "All we know is that Absolute Exterminators is using children to do their dirty work and that some of those children are being kept here at the Monroe. Nettie could be anywhere, really. And with anyone."

I know Sam is right. "Should we knock on the door?"

"No," Sam says. "It's best to hang back and watch how things work. If we go up to the door we could get pulled into trouble. Let's take our time and be smart. It can be dangerous if we're not thoughtful about our actions—both for Nettie and for the two of you."

Quinn shoves his fists into his pockets and turns his chin up to the cold night sky. His breath is a stream of white as he says, "She's just a little girl."

"Which is what makes her a perfect target," Sam says.

So we sit in the night and watch for shifting shadows or movement around the hotel.

After a while, Quinn leans his head on Sam's shoulder and yawns. "Let's go home and try again tomorrow," he says.

"Not so fast," Sam says in a low whisper as he points down the road where three more children are just leaving the hotel.

Two are boys, maybe eight or nine years old.

The third child is Nettie.

16

We slink behind piles of brick and bits of building—keeping an eye on Nettie and trailing the overseer. He is an older teenage boy who follows the three children through the streets and down to a sewer station by the river. When they get there, he gives Nettie and each boy a pouch full of something as well as an empty potato sack. He pulls three lines of rope from the pack on his back, tying one around each child's waist. Then he hands one of the boys a lantern, lifts the manhole cover in the street, and lowers them into the sewer.

"They're all alone down there," I say.

"They have the overseer, but he's just a kid, too," Sam points out. "Follow me, there's another one of these manholes around the corner."

I am wearing a green-and-red plaid dress of Ida's. When she gave it to me, she told me about her mother making it for her sixteenth birthday in Germany. "Turn away," I say, stepping into the remains of a building and crouching down behind a wall. "I can't ruin this dress."

Quinn's eyes are as wide as wheels. "You're not going into the sewer naked, are you?"

"Don't be ridiculous. I'll keep my underthings on. And I'll have my coat, which is long enough. Now turn away and keep an eye out." I slip out of the dress, tuck it carefully in a corner, and button my coat. It is shorter than I realized.

Sam whistles when I come out into the light of the street lamp. "Nice knees," he teases.

"Never mind my knees."

Quinn and I follow Sam to the other manhole cover.

"This connects to the same sewer tunnel," Sam says. "Two of us can go down but one needs to stay up here as a lookout."

"I'll go," Quinn and I both say at the same time.

Sam shakes his head as he lifts the heavy steel cover from the manhole. "I'm not about to send you two down there alone. Who knows what you'd find? I'm going. The question is, which of you will stay here to give us a hand up when it's time to come out?"

"You're stronger to help lift us out," I say to Quinn.

He must see how much I want this because he says, "Go, already."

I look into the sewer. A steamy, foul-smelling mist rises up in my face. "It's pitch-black."

"Luckily," Sam says, "I thought we might be exploring tonight and came prepared." He pulls two thick candles from his coat pocket, shimmies up the lamppost on the corner, lifts the glass, lights both of the candles, which he holds in one hand, and slides back down to the street. It is quite a feat.

"I'll go first," I say, thinking of my coat-dress and Sam being below, possibly looking up.

"There's not a ladder. You'll have to hang and then drop down. I can't guarantee you'll drop onto a platform, though that's what is usually below each of these manholes."

"How do you know so much about the sewer?" Quinn asks.

Sam grins. "They make a good getaway if you're in a bind."

"Hang and then drop," I say. "Okay." I sit on the rim of the hole and turn onto my belly. The stink is putrid and thick. I never knew you could taste a smell, but this is the kind of stench that lines your tongue and makes you want to gag.

"Now drop," Sam says from above.

I hear a light scratching of claws below. My heart starts pounding. "There's something down here."

"I know," Sam says. "Rats."

"And Nettie," Quinn adds.

I let go and drop down onto a platform. "I need a candle," I whisper up to them.

Sam ties a string around a lit candle and slowly lowers it to me. Then he lowers the second candle the same way. As soon as I hold the candles up, shadows skitter away, farther down the tunnel.

"They won't bother you if you don't bother them," Sam says, jumping down next to me. He takes one of the candles.

"So what if there are rats down here?" I ask. "Why do they have to catch them?"

"They breed in the sewers, but they're curious creatures and like to wander up into shops and homes above, where they can steal a crust of bread or a crumble of tart," Sam says. I remember Mr. Frankel teaching us how a group of rats is called a mischief and guess Sam is right. "Businesses are struggling," Sam says. "A rat infestation is enough to close down a pub or hotel." He lifts his candle up. "Walk along these ledges at the sides. They will lead us to larger platforms every so often. Pay attention and be careful not to fall in."

The ledges, as he calls them, are made of brick and are

only about ten inches wide. They run along each side of the tunnel, just above the river of sludge and slime that goes down the middle. We walk on them like we are walking a tightrope, one foot in front of the other.

"How come it's not freezing in here like it is on the street?"

"What comes out of a body is warm," Sam says. "Put enough of that together . . ."

"Oh." I don't require more details.

Looking ahead, I can see the glow of a lantern floating in the air in the distance.

Sam turns his head back to me. "Remember, we will be directly below Nettie's overseer. We don't want to get her in trouble."

I nod, though I know he can't see me.

"Haallooo," Sam says as we come upon the next platform. One of the boys is holding up the lantern and the other boy is pouring small piles of white powder where the brick ledge meets the tunnel wall. Likely poison, I guess. "Just passing through." Sam directs those words up the hole above the boy, to the overseer.

I am about to ask where Nettie is when she pops her head out of a skinny pipe in the wall. "I got three of them," she says, pulling her arm out. Three dead rats hang by their tails in her hand.

"Did you put more medicine down?" the lantern boy asks. Now that I am closer I can see he is much older than I originally thought. Small, but older.

"Yes," Nettie says, pulling herself out of the pipe, "but I don't think this medicine is working because they keep dying." It is dark, with only a lantern and our candles to light the space, but I can see that her dress is sopping wet with black sewage and her hair is knotted in masses around her head.

The lantern boy smirks. "Well, we will just have to keep trying. Doctor's orders."

Nettie looks at the dead rats in her hand. "Poor things."

"It's good we take the sick ones out, so they don't hurt the healthy ones," the boy keeps on. Then he turns to Sam and me. "Be on your way."

That makes Nettie squinch her eyes in the dark and look past the lantern boy to where we are. "Ailis!" she hollers, dropping the rats into the sludge-water below and running— as fast as she can on the ledge—toward us.

"Aw, what'd you drop them for?" the boy whines. "You know we get paid by the head. That's three cents down the drain."

The rope around their waists pulls tight. "Quit your jawing and get to work," a voice says from above.

"The brat dropped three good ones," the lantern boy hollers up the manhole.

Nettie steps onto the platform and throws her arms out wide, but the lantern boy grabs her by the neck. "Where do you think you're goin'?"

"Let her go," I say, pulling on her arm.

He just pulls at her neck harder. "No way."

Sam steps in. "You're hurting her, both of you."

I can see he is right, so I let go. The boy keeps his hand around the back of her neck.

"Did you come to help the rats, too?" Nettie asks.

"I came to find you," I say.

The boy tightens his grip and Nettie flinches. "You shouldn't have done that," she says.

"Yeah," the boy chimes in, "that was stupid. Brat Girl's got a good job working to better the city of Chicago. Isn't that right, Brat Girl?"

"Her name is Nettie."

"Whatever."

"And she belongs with us."

The boy pulls Nettie in to his side with one hand and holds the lantern up a bit higher with the other. The yellow glow of light shimmers against his skin. I swear his two front teeth are shaved into sharp points, but it might just be the way the shadows move across his face. "That's your story, but she was bought fair and square so now she stays with us."

I turn to Sam and give him a look like, *Why aren't you saying anything?* And, *What's wrong with you?* And, *What a useless bit of help you are!*

His expression is flat. "Like I said, we're just passing through. Come on, Ailis."

"I'm not going anywhere."

Sam leans in. "We don't want to cause her trouble," he says between his teeth.

"Good thinkin'," the lantern boy says, pulling on Nettie's rope. "Take the brat up, Joey." He sets his lantern down and lifts Nettie up as the older boy from above slowly pulls on her rope.

"Check on Kristina for me," Nettie says as she rises up into the air. She is like a rag doll being hauled out of the sitting hole of an outhouse. "And tell Miss Franny hello."

"I will," I promise.

"Take my advice," the lantern boy says to us, "leave her alone. You don't want the kind of trouble meddlin' causes. I've seen it and it's not pretty. If you really do care about the girl, you'll forget you ever saw her."

By the time we get up onto the street with Quinn, I can't stop shaking. Partly from coming up into the cold from the warm, vile sewer and partly because I realize Sam is right—trying to help Nettie will put her in unspeakable danger.

"We have to be careful about this," Sam says. "Sly, like a fox. What did that teacher of yours say about foxes?"

I know he is trying to lighten my mood but I shake my head, still trembling. "Nothing."

Quinn takes off his coat and wraps it around my shoulders. "You're freezing. Go change into your dress and we'll talk to the police again first thing in the morning."

"The police are as dirty as that sewer we just stepped out of," Sam says. "Chicago is notorious for corruption. The cops in this city don't care about an orphan girl. Especially if ignoring her means one of their insiders makes more money."

"What can we do?" Quinn asks.

"Watch," Sam says. "Wait. Hope to find her alone and then try to convince her to leave."

"She wants out," I say. "I could see it in her face."

"Maybe, but at what cost?" Sam puts his hand on my shoulder. "As long as she does what they want, she'll get a bowl of broth and a place to sleep. We can rest easier knowing Nettie is alive and that she listens and obeys. Our job is to keep our distance, watch for their weakness, and not cause her any unnecessary problems."

I duck away to change into Ida's dress and then follow Quinn and Sam back to the boardinghouse. At one point along the way, Quinn attempts small talk but eventually gives up and joins our silence.

When we get to the corner of Miss Franny's street, Sam says, "I think you're safe to finish on from here."

"Where are you going?" Quinn asks, and I am surprised he can't guess.

"Well," Sam says, rubbing a finger next to that crooked nose of his, "I thought I'd do a bit more inquiry about the rat extermination company over at the pub. You know, have a pint and chat a bit." He looks down at his watch. "They are pouring drinks for another hour still."

"Oh," Quinn says. The word tumbles out soft and low.

When we get back to Miss Franny's, everyone is in their rooms for the night. Quinn and I spread our blankets on the front room floor and he falls asleep right away. I sit next to him, looking at his sagging mouth and peaceful expression. What dreams happen behind those closed eyes, I wonder. How can he fall asleep so easily?

I put on my coat and shoes, grab an extra blanket, and go onto the front porch, careful to open the door slowly so the hinges don't creak and give me away. I sit in the rocker and look up at the moon. It is unadorned white—like it should be—and looking at it makes me remember the moon on the night of our Peshtigo fire. How it glowed a sickly red-orange color. And how the sky was so heavy with ash it made gray, splotchy patterns across that cinnamon moon.

As much as I hate that memory, what I hate even more is the way the fire moon turned back to white the very next night. As if nothing had happened. As if all was as it should be again.

I shiver from the cold and pull my knees up under the blanket, wrapping the corner ends around my ankles. I hum one of Mother's songs and count money in my head, trying to figure out how much we have saved and how much more we need. I do whatever I can to ignore the sense of hopelessness that lines the bottom of my soul and makes me ache in the deepest part of my bones.

Soon I hear Sam clomping up the front walkway, singing a parlor tune about a barmaid with red curls.

When he sees me, he slaps his hand across his mouth and says, "Excuse me, dearest one."

Miss Franny must have heard him as well because she swings the door open and clicks her tongue. "Sam Abbott, whatever will I do with you?"

"What a lovely belle you are," Sam says, leaning forward and spitting as he speaks.

"You're drunk again." She places his arm around her neck and pulls him inside. But not before she gives me a look like it's all somehow my fault.

I rub my face and pull the blanket around my shoulders. I am exhausted, so I go inside and curl up next to Quinn on the floor. Still, sleep doesn't come. I lie there thinking of Nettie until morning light bleeds through the edges of the front room curtain and then I get up, knowing I need to do something more. Knowing it's time to talk to Mr. Olsen again.

17

Once our chores are complete and Quinn is playing his fiddle in the bazaar, I go to Ida's and ask if I can take the day off to visit Mr. Olsen. Quinn would be upset if he knew my plans to go without him but something in me needs to be alone. I want to walk the streets and feel anonymous and not have to explain where I am going or what I am thinking. I tell myself Chicago is safe when the sun is out and the streets are crowded.

"Of course, *Liebling*," Ida says. "I can go with you."

"You shouldn't close the store because of me. It's something I want to do alone."

She pushes her lips together and nods slowly. "Okay, I will let you do this thing you need to do. But you must tell me if I can help, yes?"

I start for the door. "I'll be back tomorrow."

I head out on Canal Street and through the ruined part of the city. I slow when I come upon the section where the man in the piano box had been. The box is still there in the middle of the sidewalk and he is slumped up against it, sleeping. People walk around him as if he doesn't exist. As if they see grown men sleeping in big wooden piano boxes every day of their lives.

I take the dime I brought for lunch from my pocket, ease up to where he is sleeping, and set it quietly by his side— knowing someone could possibly steal the money, but not wanting to wake him up.

He snorts and I jump. But then he crosses his arms, snuggles deeper into his coat, and keeps sleeping.

I walk on to North Avenue, turn left, and keep going until I am standing in front of those massive black gates. Like before, I ring the call bell.

"Yes?" the butler says from the doorway at the other end of the walk.

"It's Ailis Doyle to see Mr. Olsen."

"Mr. Olsen is not in."

It feels odd hollering down the path, but the gate is locked and the butler isn't budging from the front door. "Can I come back later?"

"You may, but Mr. Olsen will still be out."

"When do you expect him?"

Finally, the butler comes away from the door and out to where I am standing. "It is not my place to say, but I know the master has an interest where you and your brother are concerned."

"Thank you."

"Mr. Olsen has left Chicago to work on matters regarding the railway line he is building. He will not return for another week."

"A week! I need to speak to him about something very important. I need his help."

The butler raises both hands. "I have no control in this matter. He is a busy man and often gone."

"Can you telegraph him somehow?"

"I am sorry," the butler says. "I will let Mr. Olsen know you inquired when he returns."

"Can you tell him we've learned what happened to Nettie? The orphan girl who was staying at his boardinghouse. She's been forced into the rat trade."

He hesitates, clearly taken aback by the news. "I will relay the message as soon as possible. Now, good day." He turns back up the walk and disappears behind the broad doors.

Mr. Olsen is the only person I thought might be able to convince the police to investigate Absolute Exterminators. Without him at my side, I'm afraid no one will listen. I begin walking down North Avenue, back into Chicago's rubble. I walk without thinking and without feeling. I am numb on the outside from December's icy air and numb on the inside from the bleak and bitter truth surrounding me.

I press on down Canal Street and stop on the corner of Monroe. In the afternoon light, I can see Sam was right; two men sit guard out front of the hotel, playing cards on an overturned box, and another leans up against the corner of the building.

I can also see an outhouse behind the hotel. It stands fifteen or twenty feet from the back door.

Unsupervised.

I walk over to Madison Street and approach the hotel from behind to avoid the guards. A boy is coming out the rear door of the hotel as I sneak up.

"Psst," I whisper, hiding behind the outhouse.

He rubs his eyes and yawns.

"Psst," I say again, only a little sharper and louder.

That gets his attention. He starts to speak but I put my finger to my lips and then crook the other hand, asking him over to where I am crouching down.

"Who are you?" he asks when he gets to the outhouse.

"A friend of Nettie's. Is she inside?"

"Maybe."

"Can you get her for me?"

His eyes flit to the hotel. "No."

"Why not?"

"I ain't gonna get beat on account of a snot-nosed girl."

I reach into my coat pocket and pull out a penny. "All you have to do is tell her to come outside."

His eyes are fixed on the penny. "She's still sleeping."

"Wake her up and tell her to use the outhouse. That's all I'm asking." I push the penny out a bit farther.

He snaps it up from my palm in a flash and then steps back, as if I will do something to him for taking it.

"It's okay," I say. "I'm a friend."

"No such thing," he mutters as he tucks the penny into his pocket and flees into the hotel.

I wait for what seems like forever before the door is pushed open and Nettie steps out. "Hello?" she says into the empty yard.

I poke my head out from the back of the outhouse and smile but then wave my arms and point over to the side of the hotel where I know the thugs are, warning her to be quiet.

She gets the picture and creeps over to where I am hiding. When she gets there, I notice her eyelids are red and bloated. "What happened to you?" I ask. Nettie shrugs and presses her fists to her eyes. I grab her hands and see they are caked with dirt—and that the crevices of filth are lined with white powder. "This is rat poison," I say, trying to keep my voice down. "You're getting it in your eyes."

"It's rat *medicine*," she says. "Why are you here?"

"I want you to come back to Miss Franny's with me. We miss you."

Nettie shakes her head, eyes wide as she can get them. "Can't," she whispers.

"Yes, you can. Sneak away with me right now."

"It's not safe. They'll get you and Quinn and Kristina and even Miss Franny."

"They're just trying to scare you. Come on, let's go." I tug on her arm but she pulls it back and sits down.

"Look what I found." She reaches into her pinafore pocket and pulls out a handful of trinkets. "Treasure," she says, "buried under the streets." She lines the items up on the ground and motions for me to sit down. "Look at this ribbon, isn't it pretty?"

It is filthy, tattered, and only about two inches long.

"And I found this sparkly rock and this pink comb with only a few broken teeth and then I found this actual tooth." She points to a decaying molar sitting next to the comb. "Isn't that lucky? Finding a broken-tooth comb and then a tooth on the same day?"

Nettie has always been naïve and ignoring trouble is how

she copes with difficult things. Still, she seems different as I watch her point out these bits of trash in front of me. She is stroking the ribbon on the ground with her finger and I notice the edge of a dark blue bruise on her arm, just under her sleeve. I point to the rim of the bruise. "They're hurting you."

She pulls her sleeve down and scoops up her treasures. "Thanks for visiting me. Please don't come back."

"Nettie."

She shakes her head and runs into the hotel. I want to grab her or holler after her, but she's already gone and I don't want to bring the overseer-thug-guards around, which wouldn't be good for anyone.

• • •

Quinn is sitting on the bed of a parked wagon in front of Miss Franny's, his fiddle on his lap. I expect him to yell at me the moment he sees my face coming his way, but he waits until I get right in front of him and then says, "I was worried about you."

"Sorry," I say. I was ready for a quarrel. I had figured out my side of the argument about how I am the oldest and how if I want to spend a day doing something by myself then I shouldn't have to get his permission. How Nettie is more my responsibility than anyone else's and how I need to sort things out in my mind. I am not prepared for somber Quinn. For sad Quinn. "Let's go inside," I say.

"We can't."

"What do you mean?" I ask.

"I was late getting back to do my chores because I was out looking for you and Miss Franny got in a huff, saying we've been skipping and skimping on our work for too many days and she's tired of us not doing anything and then she said I was just another lazy Irish Mick."

I can tell there is more to his story so I ask, "And what did you say back to her?"

"I told her she was a wretched old witch and that she could chop her own wood once in a while."

A laugh jumps out of my mouth.

Quinn goes on. "Then she said maybe a night on the cold streets will make us appreciate her hospitality. She probably didn't mean it but I was so mad I left anyway. Now I just don't want to deal with her."

"I don't blame you," I say.

I climb up onto the wagon bed next to him.

We sit side by side and let the last wisp of daylight sink down into the earth. I tell Quinn about Nettie and he suggests we bring a bucket of water for her to wash her hands and face. It is a good idea and I am grateful for the suggestion. "And food," I add. "She looked hungry."

A light snow starts to fall, barely, but it keeps coming down, building a thin veil of wet across our heads and coats. "We can't stay here all night," Quinn says out of the quiet. "Maybe we could ask Ida if we could bunk with her."

"I don't want to bother her so late. Besides, her apartment is so small. You've seen it, it's just one little room. What do you think about going in to Miss Franny's?"

"I'm not ready to apologize," he says. "Not after what she called me."

"I have an idea." I lead him around the side of the boarding-house to the chicken coop. "I know it's clean because I just changed the straw."

"Miss Franny won't like it," Quinn says.

"Who's going to tell?"

Quinn is considering the idea and says, "At least we'll be out of this snow. And Kristina's not there to peck at us. The other hens are a lot nicer than Kristina."

"Rattlesnakes are nicer than Kristina," I say, leading the way into the coop.

Quinn follows me as I pluck out slimy pieces of chicken poop from the egg beds and pile the clean straw against one side of the small henhouse. "It's not so bad," he says. "It's softer than Miss Franny's floor."

"But a lot colder out here."

"At least we have each other."

It is something Father often said when times were rough.

Quinn is becoming more like him every day. Maybe it is the fiddle; I don't know, but it's nice to be around. I try to add to the optimism: "Can't get any worse."

"I guess you're right," Quinn says, but we both know those words are hollow. If there is one thing we've learned over the past eleven weeks it is that things can always get worse.

We awake at dawn the next morning nestled in straw and cuddled by chickens. It wasn't as horrible a night as I thought it would be.

"Guess I should apologize to Miss Franny so we can get started on her chore list," Quinn says.

"I don't think you should. Mr. Olsen doesn't expect us to be her slaves, he said so himself."

"Mr. Olsen isn't here and we can't keep sleeping with the chickens."

"Why not?" I ask. "Think about it, Quinn, we will be free of Miss Franny. We can spend more time trying to help Nettie or working to build our savings and then sneak in here after dark and have a soft bed in this straw. It's not forever, it's just for now."

"That might be nice," he says, pulling a piece of yellow straw from his hair.

"No more of her insults."

"Unless we get caught," he says. "In which case we'd really be in for it."

"We won't get caught," I promise.

"Will we let Sam know?"

"I'm afraid he'd tell. Not on purpose, but he might slip and say something when he's had one too many down at the pub. Which is every night."

"So we just let him think we've disappeared?"

I know that won't work. Sam cares for us and would worry. "Give me time to think about it. Right now we need to get out of here before Miss Franny finds us." Quinn pushes a gray hen off his lap. She screeches and flaps her wings in my face. "Be careful," I say, pushing her back toward the nesting box. "Her talons are sharp."

"I guess there'll be no oatmeal for us this morning," Quinn says.

"No, but we've got fresh eggs." I hold two up in my hands.

"How are we to cook them?"

I smack the end of one egg against the corner of the nesting box and then put the broken part to my lips, sucking out the thick, warm innards.

"That's disgusting," Quinn says.

"It's breakfast and it's all we have." I hold the other egg out to Quinn.

"I'm not about to suck on a raw egg. Let's go get something at Quixom's."

I put my empty shell in my pocket. "I don't want to leave any evidence we were here and Mr. Frankel says eggshells are full of healthy minerals."

"Said."

"What?"

"Mr. Frankel *said*. He can't talk anymore."

"I know," I say.

"And I don't care how hungry I get. I'm not eating raw eggs or their shells. I'd rather play on the streets for an extra hour and earn money for food."

I know there is no stopping him so we take a bucket from Miss Franny's shed, walk a few blocks over to Quixom's Market and buy three sandwiches for breakfast. Mine is egg and Cheddar cheese on rye bread with hot mustard. It is soft and spicy and scrumptious. Then we fill the bucket with water at the corner pump and go to the Monroe.

The same two guards are out front, but the guy who had been at the side of the building is gone.

"We have to come in from behind, on Madison," I say. Quinn lets me take the lead. He is carrying his fiddle in one hand and the bucket in the other. "We wait here," I whisper when we get to the outhouse. "I need a penny to bribe her out."

Quinn gives me a penny.

After about twenty minutes or so, the boy I talked to before comes out.

"Psst," I say.

He smiles and holds out his hand. I drop the penny onto his palm and say, "Go get her."

"Anyone who would pay a penny to see someone would probably pay two."

"That's extortion."

He shrugs. "I call it good business."

I look at Quinn, who hands me another penny. "Fine." I give it to the boy, who closes his hand around the money.

"Wait here," he says.

"And keep it quiet," I whisper after him as he goes inside.

Nettie comes out within just a few minutes. Her brow is furrowed and her chin is tucked down. "I told you not to come back."

"We brought you a sandwich," I say.

"And fresh water," Quinn adds, pulling the bucket from its hiding spot behind the outhouse.

She drops down to her knees and pushes her face into the bucket of water, drinking so deeply, she starts to cough.

"Slowly," I say.

"It tastes good," she says between gulps.

"When's the last time you had fresh water?" Quinn asks.

"We're not allowed to go to the main pump and the pipes are busted here," she answers, still drinking. "The only water we get is down below."

"Sewer water?"

"Some of it's clean," she says. "And you can get the helpers to bring you a cup of water if you give them pennies."

"You mean the kidnappers," Quinn clarifies.

I notice she is eyeing the sandwich on my lap. "Go ahead, it's for you." I fold back the brown paper and hand it to her.

She keeps her face down, shoving one bite after another into her cheeks like a squirrel going into the worst of winter. I take the opportunity of her distraction to say a few things. "Listen, Nettie," I begin, "these people are lying to you and they have no power to hurt us if you leave."

She flits her eyes up to me, but keeps eating. She is forcing the sandwich in faster than she can chew and bits of bread and cheese are dropping out of the corners of her mouth.

"You could come home with us right now and no one here would notice or care."

"Tell that to Markie," she says, mouth overflowing.

"Who's Markie?"

She stops and swallows. "A boy who ran. They found him and beat him up real bad. Tied him to a post for three days and let all the kids here spit on him." She swallows again and looks back down to the ground. "I didn't spit on him."

"Of course you didn't," I say.

"But most of the other kids did. Markie says he's sorry he ran and told us all never, ever, ever to try anything like that. Now he works harder than anyone. Now he's one of their best workers. But it sure was sad seeing him tied up like that."

Quinn dips the corner of his shirt into the water and begins wiping the mud and traces of rat poison from her free hand. "We'd keep you hidden away," he says, his voice certain. "They won't find you."

"They find whoever they want to find," she says, finishing the last crust of her sandwich. "And I'm the only one small enough to fit into some parts of the sewer. They need me."

"We need you!" I say.

Quinn puts his finger to his lips, reminding me about the thugs out front.

"We need you," I say again, only quieter.

She lets Quinn finish washing her hands and then she plunges them into the bucket and scoops the cold, fresh water onto her eyes. She does that three times and then looks up at us. "I shouldn't have eaten that whole sandwich. I should have shared it with the others. They're hungry, too."

"It's okay," Quinn says. "We'll bring more tomorrow."

"Really?" Her face lights up.

"Sure," he says.

"What are you talking about?" I say. "There's not going to be a tomorrow because she's coming with us right now!" I can't help raising my voice with each word and, by the end, the two thugs from the front are rounding the corner into the backyard. Nettie stands up and runs as fast as she can, disappearing into the hotel.

"Come on," Quinn says, grabbing the bucket and his fiddle. "They look like they mean business, we'd better run."

Leaving Nettie behind makes me feel like we are a couple of rats ourselves. And maybe we are. A couple of rats scurrying back into Chicago's nameless crowds.

• • •

Once we are far enough away from the hotel, Quinn and I stop to catch our breath.

"I'm so glad we ran into you," a woman says, coming up to us on the street. Then she turns to a well-dressed man at her side and says, "This is the musician I was telling you about."

Quinn stops and leans forward into a grand bow. He is still carrying the bucket in one hand and his fiddle in the other. "Good morning," he says, sounding amazingly mature and professional. "Do you have a request?"

The man sizes Quinn up and turns to the woman. "He's a street urchin."

"A gifted street urchin," she says. "Let him play."

"Do you know any Beethoven, boy?"

"No, sir."

"Vivaldi?"

"What I know, I learned from my father," Quinn says. "Irish jigs and a few English ditties. Nothing classical."

The man gives the woman a look of exasperation. "What current musician of worth doesn't know Beethoven or Vivaldi?"

"Stop being so stuffy, Robert," the woman says. "Put aside your judgment and let the boy play."

The man pulls out a gold pocket watch, flips it open, closes it with a *snap*, and says, "Fine. Play what you will."

Quinn blows on his fingers to warm them, opens his case, and tunes his fiddle. Then he starts playing a heartbreak of a song with lingering notes that reach deep into your soul and tease out all the emotion. The man is clearly taken by my brother's performance and, upon the last note, begins to raise his hands to clap but Quinn breaks into a lightning-fast jig that bounces out across the street and down the rooftops.

The woman leans in to the man and I hear her say, "Some play music and others play memories. This boy plays memories and it haunts me somehow."

"Chicago is full of street musicians, as is New York and every other city in the world," he says.

"There is more to this boy. There is heart and promise."

The man inclines his chin ever so slightly. "Perhaps you are right."

"I am always right," the woman says as Quinn finishes his set of songs. "What is your name, boy?"

"Quinn Doyle."

"Have you a home?"

"No, ma'am."

"Is this your sister?"

"Yes, ma'am."

"Do you know who this man at my side is? He is Robert Donlope, director of Chicago's Grand School of Music. I am Gayle Shumway, his secretary. Give the boy your calling card, Robert."

Mr. Donlope hands Quinn a card along with a five-dollar bill. "For your music and, if I may suggest, a bath."

"Thank you kindly," Quinn says.

Miss Shumway smiles. "You should know Mr. Donlope

reserves his calling card for the most important of people. Do consider paying him a visit."

Quinn just stands there, jaw hanging open, so I say, "Yes, ma'am, he certainly will."

The pair walk on and I nudge Quinn. "Wow."

"I know!" he says. "Five dollars for two songs!"

"Five dollars and a calling card. When will you go see him?"

Quinn tucks the cash into his pocket and tosses the calling card into the gutter. "We don't have money for a school like that. I can hardly read."

"You don't need to be good at reading to learn music."

"Count me out."

But as he walks down the street, I take the card from the gutter.

"We can buy a dozen sandwiches with this money and still have some left over," he says when I catch up with him. "Who is so rich they can drop five dollars for two songs?"

"And a bath," I add.

Quinn stops on the sidewalk. "I played near a bathhouse a few days ago. The sign said it was ten cents for shared water and twenty cents for fresh. Let's go there after work today."

"If we had Nettie, she could come, too. She really needs a bath."

"She was right when she said those thugs at the hotel

would come looking for her," Quinn says. "And that the punishment would be worse than anything she's going through now."

"So we just leave her there?"

"Of course not. But like Sam said, we have to be smart in how we go about it. Maybe we can save Nettie and help the other kids, too."

"Shut the whole place down?" I ask.

"They'd all be free—and safe."

"How?"

Quinn looks wearily down the street. "That's the part we have to figure out. In the meantime, we can bring her food and water and try to talk to her. If she wants to run, we'll be there."

Every beat of my heart and pulse of my veins wants to lure Nettie out, grab her, and take off. I am sure she'd understand once we got her away from those people. We could try to keep her hidden. But maybe Quinn and Sam are right. As long as Mr. Blume's lackeys were looking for her, she'd never be safe. As long as she *wants* to stay—even for the wrong reasons—I'll be unable to force her into hiding.

"It's going to take patience," Quinn says. "In the meantime, we need to take care of ourselves. It's like Mother said—if we don't take care of ourselves, how can we care for others?"

"That wasn't Mother. That was Nettie quoting one of the nuns from her orphanage."

Quinn's expression falls. "It hasn't even been three months and I'm already forgetting them."

I take the bucket from his left hand. "Mixing up something they said is not forgetting them. I'll never let you forget and you'll never let me forget. Maybe that's why we both survived."

Quinn pinches his eyebrows together and says, "Maybe."

I look up at the sky. "Ida's expecting me. Where will you play?"

"By the cobbler's shop," he says. "In the bazaar, where it's warm."

"Down from Ketchum's Butcher Shop?"

"Yes." I can tell he's still thinking about mixing up Mother's memory.

I force a smile. "Play to remember them today and I'll meet you there at three o'clock."

He nods and disappears into the crowd.

• • •

After work, I follow Quinn across the city to a hotel with an adjacent bathhouse. It is surprisingly clean. Some bathhouses have bad reputations, but this place seems respectable.

"I want fresh water," I say.

"Me too." Quinn hands me two dimes and waves me ahead of him in line. "I'll see you when you get out."

I follow an attendant into the back room. It is small but nice and the dividing walls between the baths go from the floor all the way up to the ceiling, which makes me feel more comfortable. The attendant, a young girl with a blond braid and white apron, hands me a towel. "Soap is along the ledge."

"Thank you."

She leaves me alone to slip out of my dress and into the bath. The water is steamy and warm. Even when we bathed on the farm, the water was always cold. I slide down into the tub and let the water ease up around my shoulders and neck, closing my eyes. The sorrow I have been carrying for so long begins melting from my skin, along with the dirt. I imagine it lifting off and dissolving into the warm water and I stay in the bath until the last trace of warmth fades away. When I finally get out, I feel so light. Like I could be the Ailis I once was.

Oh, how I want to be that Ailis.

I get dressed, twist my hair into a fresh braid, and go out into the alley to meet Quinn.

"You look like a new person," he says.

"I feel like a new person."

He nods. "Yeah, I do, too. It's good."

"I'm tired of being sad," I say. "But it doesn't feel right being happy when I remember all we've lost and the trouble Nettie is in."

"I know what you mean. I've been feeling bad about going to the bonfire with Sam and dancing around like a fool. I just couldn't stop myself."

"Mother and Father wouldn't want us to be sad forever."

"How long is long enough?" he asks. It is a good question and I don't know the answer so I shrug. Quinn picks up his fiddle and I pick up the bucket.

"Maybe it's when you can't stand to carry the weight of it anymore," I say when we are down the road a ways. "When you feel like the sorrow is changing who you are meant to be."

"Is that how you're feeling?" he asks.

I think about it. "Yes."

"Then you shouldn't. We'll figure out a way to help Nettie. Instead of thinking of her in a sad way, try to think of a way to get her out."

"I wish I could."

"Maybe it's something you do one minute at a time. And let's make a pact," he says, reaching out a hand. "From now on, we only talk about the good times back home, okay?"

I slide my hand into his and shake it. "Like how Gertrude used to chase the chickens around the yard?"

"Flapping her arms and clucking at them?"

I laugh. "She was the cutest thing." The memory makes us smile, but murky sadness lingers, waiting to crawl back in and choke our hearts with gloom. We both know our sorrow won't disappear by recalling one funny memory. But for the first time since the fires, I feel peace in knowing Quinn and I can at least talk about our family.

19

Ida told me she was meeting a carpenter to design a new hat block and would be opening the shop an hour later than usual today, which works out nicely with our plan to take Nettie and the other children some sandwiches. Another night in Miss Franny's chicken coop with our light coats makes Quinn suggest we stop by the church on our way and ask if there have been any coat donations.

When we get there, Father Farlane leads us to a rear corner of the church. "We have plenty of offerings," he says. "There has been such generosity since our city's tragedy. As terrible as these situations are, they sometimes bring out the best in people. Wouldn't you agree?"

I wouldn't—not after all I've seen.

"Any word on your friend?" Father Farlane asks, pulling a wool coat from the box and holding it up to Quinn. "This might fit you."

"Sort of," I say. "We learned she was stolen off the streets and is working in the sewers, killing rats."

"Terrible news," he says.

"They've scared her," I say. "And we can't convince her to run."

"That is often the case in these matters. It's a sad truth of our times and one the system seems to support."

Quinn drops his old coat into the box and slips his arms into the sleeves of the heavier one. "We can't fix everything, but we want to help Nettie escape."

"Definitely," I agree.

Father Farlane's eyes soften with his smile. "I wish I had more time to help. My duties since the fire have kept me so busy. I will keep the matter in my personal prayers."

That seems pointless. I dig to the bottom of the box and realize there aren't any ladies' coats so I pull out a wide-breasted navy coat. It will have to do. "Thank you," I say. "Can we bring one of these coats for Nettie?"

"Of course," Father Farlane says. "Though I don't see any that would fit a child her size."

"This might work." I pull a boy's coat out. It is faded and three sizes too big, but at least it will be warm. I imagine her burrowing into it like a field mouse in a woolen blanket.

"Excellent," Father Farlane says. "If that is all you need—"

"Would you say a prayer with us, Father?" Quinn asks, which stuns me.

I start to explain how completely unnecessary that is, but Father Farlane agrees before I have a chance to gather my words. He takes our hands and starts in fervent prayer. Quinn's head is down but I can't bring myself to participate. I look around at the cold stone walls of the church and think of Ida's question: *Where is God in these moments?* When Father Farlane finishes, he gives my hand a squeeze and thanks us for coming to see him.

"We just needed warm coats," I say, causing Quinn to give me a dirty look that I don't understand.

"Thank you again, Father," Quinn says pointedly, as if I am somehow being ungrateful.

"Of course," Father Farlane says, putting his hands into the pocket slits of his robe and walking down the hallway.

"What?" I say to Quinn's look when we are alone again at the back of the church.

"Forget it. Let's go get those sandwiches."

So we go to Quixom's Market and buy as many sandwiches as we can with the remaining money the music school man gave us—which turns out to be fourteen sandwiches. At first, Mr. Quixom smirks at our order but the moment Quinn puts the four dollars and fifty cents upon his countertop, the shop owner gets this wide, sloppy grin on his face and begins slicing bread. Then we tromp through the slushy streets to the main water pump to fill Miss Franny's bucket once again.

"Not so high it sloshes over," I admonish, tying Nettie's new coat around my waist to free my hands.

"I know," Quinn says.

I kick at a pile of dirty snow that looks like a sad, wilted mountain and imagine how Nettie's face will look when she sees we brought fourteen sandwiches. I can't guess how many children are held up in that hotel, but Mr. Quixom has been generous with the egg-and-cheese filling. Even if they share them, it will still make a decent meal. Not to mention having a new coat for her. I push the toe of my shoe along the jagged edge of the snow pile and ask Quinn, "Do you remember that story Father sometimes told if he found us lazing at our work?"

"About the children sleeping on the sunny rocks?"

It was a warning about an area in Ireland—near Rosses Point—where the sun shone down on a small patch of rounded rocks. If children allowed themselves to be lured by the warmth and fell asleep, fairies would slink in and steal their wits and the children would wake up fool-headed. "Yes," I say. "I thought of that story when I saw Nettie yesterday."

"She's not fool-headed," Quinn says, stopping in the street.

"I know, but she wasn't herself either. She's allowed them to get inside her mind and convince her they are helping the rats and saving the city. Did you hear how she called those guards *helpers*? Does she really think they are helping her?"

"Maybe she has to be that way to survive," Quinn says. "I think that's always been the case with Nettie, but more so now."

I fall in step with him, carrying the bucket of water and trying to keep it from sloshing over.

We turn onto Madison Street and cut across the rubble to the back of the Monroe Hotel. We aren't there two minutes when that same boy comes sauntering out the rear door.

"Thought I'd see you again," he says, wrapping his fingers around his shabby gray suspenders. Then he sees the bucket of water. "I'll take a drink instead of a penny."

"We brought sandwiches, too," Quinn whispers, leaning his fiddle against the back of the outhouse and raising the package from Quixom's Market.

"Swell!" the boy says.

"Shhh!" I warn, remembering the guards just around the front of the building. I want to give Nettie a sandwich first but I can't find it in me to turn this hungry boy away. "Be quick," I say, stepping aside and letting him kneel down at the bucket.

He drinks deeply and then takes a sandwich from Quinn, ramming it into his mouth, hardly chewing at all.

"Now go get Nettie," I say when he is almost done. "And don't say anything about these sandwiches. I want her to be the one to give them to the other kids."

He ignores me until he has eaten the last bit of bread and pushed his face back into the bucket, taking two more long drinks.

"Go get her," I say again when he is done.

"Can't." He drags his sleeve across his mouth and face, making a pink streak of clean on one cheek. "She ain't here no more."

"What do you mean?" Quinn asks. "Is she working?"

"Maybe she's working, maybe she's sleeping. Whatever she's doing, it ain't at this hideout. After they saw you visiting her yesterday, they tied her up and took her off."

"Where?" I demand. "And what do you mean, they tied her up?"

"Ankles together, wrists together, and then a rope from the ankles to the wrists. Like a proper hog."

My mouth falls open and I look to Quinn. I notice his hands are trembling.

"If you brought those sandwiches for us," the boy says, stepping toward the package, "I can take them inside."

Quinn's right arm snaps out and grabs the boy by a twist of his collar. He pulls the boy in to his face, nose to dirty nose, and says, "Listen here." The words leak out between Quinn's teeth and even I am scared. I've never seen him like this before. "You're gonna find out where they took Nettie and you're gonna tell us, understand?"

The boy doesn't answer so Quinn shakes him good and strong and pulls him back nose to nose. "Do you understand?"

The boy makes a fragile squeaking noise and shakes his head. "They'll never tell me where she is."

Quinn's rage is pulsing just below his skin. Red splotches creep up his neck and across his cheeks. "Nettie is an innocent girl. If you don't help her, I'll make you sorry you ever lived a day on this earth." He drops the boy, landing him on his bottom. "We'll be back," he says as he picks up his fiddle.

I look at Quinn and then down at the boy, who is on the ground. My brother's actions astound me and my heart is flapping around my chest like a wild bird in a cage, but I wonder if it had the same effect on this boy. He is probably used to being pushed around. "We need your help," I say in the most imploring way I can, though the plea seems meaningless in the wake of Quinn's threats.

The boy scrambles over, grabs the Quixom's package, and darts back into the hotel.

Quinn is stunned by his own outburst and starts walking with a listless gait. At least, I am guessing him to be stunned. Maybe he is upset at the dreadful turn of events for Nettie. I walk in silence at his side, still holding Nettie's new coat and toting the empty bucket I dumped out after the boy ran back into the hotel. The red splotches on Quinn's neck begin to lighten and fade away.

I feel something wet land upon my nose and look up. Dark clouds are stealing across the sky, spitting out slushy snowflakes and blocking any trace of sunlight.

We go to Ida's shop because it is fairly close, but the door is locked and the CLOSED sign is hanging behind the glass.

"She won't be back for a little while still," I say. "She was going to meet that carpenter, remember?"

"Where's the carpenter's shop?"

"I don't know," I admit, worried about Ida in this storm. She doesn't have a wagon, so she would have walked or taken a hansom cab.

"Wherever she is," Quinn says, "she'll have to stay until this passes." He tries Ida's door once more, then starts off in the direction of Miss Franny's. It is clear he is still pretty shaken by what happened at the Monroe.

As we walk, the snow quickly turns from small, wet flakes into heavy sheets of freezing slush. Wind appears out of nowhere and what began as a reasonably bright morning quickly spirals down into the wicked darkness of an Illinois blizzard.

My eyes are fixed on Quinn's new coat a few feet ahead of me and I think to reach out and grab the hem to keep from losing him (or him from losing me) but can't coax my free hand out of its pocket. I am enveloped by frozen misery and by the time we start down Miss Franny's street, I can hardly feel any of my limbs.

"There's someone on the porch," Quinn says as we get to Miss Franny's. It's hard to hear him through the storm. "How are we gonna sneak into the henhouse?"

Before I can think of an answer, the figure on the porch comes running down toward us. It is Sam.

"Where have you been?"

"Miss Franny kicked us out," I say, knowing that isn't exactly why we are caught in the storm but taking the opportunity to help Sam see the light.

"She never expected you to stay away," Sam says. "She was just angry. The truth is, she's been pacing the floor with worry." He puts his arm around Quinn's shoulder. "We've been lookin' all over for you two." The yowling wind slices Sam's words and I wonder how air can be so loud.

"They took her away," I say through the storm. "We went to visit Nettie, but a boy there said they tied her up and took her somewhere else."

Sam pulls me in with his other arm and gives my shoulder a gentle squeeze. "We'll find her," he says. "I promise."

I tuck my chin down to avoid the bitter-cold snow as Sam guides us into Miss Franny's.

The residents there are milling around the main room, where a fire blazes in the great stone fireplace. It is the only grand thing about the home, and when it is lit, it is majestic.

"You found them!" a woman says when Sam brings us in. I don't recognize her, but Quinn and I are discouraged from interacting with the paying customers. Not that I am interested, anyway. There are so many of them and they are always changing. The woman looks out the window. "And just in time. It's dreadful out there."

Quinn strips off his coat, drops it in a crumpled heap, and sits down in front of the fire. I want to join him but know Miss Franny would have a word to say about wet coats on the floor. So I pick up Quinn's coat and go into the kitchen to hang it on one of the allotted nails by the back door.

That's where Miss Franny is. She isn't pacing the floor

like Sam said; she is slouching on a stool in the far corner, shoving a muffin into her mouth. When she sees me, she puts the remaining muffin down and says, "Well, well. If it isn't the prodigal child crawling back home."

"Sam made us come." I hang Quinn's coat on a nail, along with the new one we got for Nettie. "And this isn't my home."

"I see you are still an ungrateful rat," she says.

"And I see you are still a miserable codfish."

Sam is at the kitchen door. "You promised not to argue, Fran. It's been a tough day for Ailis. We knew where they were hiding Nettie but Ailis just found out the girl has been moved somewhere different. Take it easy on her."

"That snot called me a codfish!"

Sam's head drops into his hands and he rubs his face with a low moan. I imagine he would give anything to be at the pub just now. "You two ladies need to get along," he says through his hands. Then he looks at us. His eyes are dull and tired. "Please?" he asks.

Miss Franny tugs on her apron. "Fine," she says as if she is granting a favor. "I'm sorry to hear about Nettie. I truly am. I understand this has been difficult for you, Ailis, so I will do my best to forgive your cruel words and overlook your dismal nature." She gives a short nod to Sam, who sighs and leaves the room.

"Wow, thanks," I say.

"If you truly wish to thank me, you will begin by scrubbing these pots. The plates and cups are also in need of washing."

"But the water pump is outside. In the storm."

She gives me a hard look so I go outside.

The snow is sharp with bits of ice and the wind blows it sideways. It feels like miniature knives slicing my cheeks and ears as I get water for Miss Franny's dishes. Luckily, the pump isn't frozen over, but the handle is painfully cold and I tremble uncontrollably as I pour the water into a pot and wait for it to warm on the stove. After a few minutes, Quinn thaws out enough to realize I'm not there and comes into the kitchen to check on me.

"You should go in the other room where it's warmer," he says. "You're gonna get sick if you don't warm up."

"Which would suit Miss Franny just fine. She'll be easy to spot at my funeral. Just look for the person dancing a jig."

"That's not funny."

"Who said I was joking?" I hold my hands close to the stove and then rub them together. It hurts when I try to bend my fingers, which means they are starting to thaw out. "There are so many dishes here, I'll need more than one bucket of water to get them all clean."

"I'll get more."

Quinn takes the bucket, puts on his coat, and heads outside.

Sam comes into the kitchen and swipes a muffin from the basket on the window ledge. He is the only one in the house, besides Miss Franny, who has access to the food.

"Quinn went to the pump," I tell him. "I'll finish these dishes as soon as he's back."

"No worries." Sam tosses me his muffin, which I let fall to the floor.

"I can't eat that. Queen Franny would have a fit."

Sam bends down and picks the muffin up. His blond curls bounce with the movement. "Ease up, will ya, Ailis?"

"She says the worst things to us."

"Wasn't it you who called her a codfish?"

I look away.

"You can't go around calling people names. You're too old for that sort of nonsense. It's childish and you need to be thinking more about growing up."

"What do you know about growing up?"

"You're right," he says, taking my hand and placing the muffin on my palm. "I'm a lousy adult. But that doesn't mean you should be one, too. Take this, please."

I push it back into his hands. "I'm not hungry."

"Your choice. But know Fran is sorry for what she did. And to prove it, she wants you and Quinn to move back into the rear bedroom from now on. She's agreed not to rent it out."

"You mean the closet?"

"It's a bed, isn't it?" Then he slumps down on a stool and says, "Not everyone can be as strong as you are, Ailis. Some of us splinter against the blows of this life."

I am struck. "I'm not strong."

"Are you kidding me? You're a fortress." He starts rolling the muffin against his palm. "There are things about Fran you don't know."

"Like what?"

"Like how her *supposed* mother ditched her while she was standing in a breadline when she was only four years old. Told her she was going to read the sign at the front to see when the doors opened, and asked Fran to stay and hold their place in line. But she never came back. Can you imagine how little Fran felt standing there all alone— probably for hours? And at what point she realized she had been abandoned? You grew up with parents to teach you right from wrong," he says. "But Fran grew up on the streets, all alone. Her ideas about some things, including the Irish, are wrong. I understand that. She just doesn't know any better."

I realize he intends for me to feel sorry for Miss Franny, but I can't muster anything more than a few drops of annoyance. "And that gives her the right to be mean the rest of her days?"

"Splintered," he says. "Sharp, jagged splinters where a whole person used to be. If you bothered to get to know her, you'd see she's not as bad as you think. She really has been searching for Nettie and was genuinely worried about you and Quinn. She's just lousy at showing it."

I let out a harrumph of disagreement and disgust.

"Why do you insist on only seeing the bad in her?" Sam asks.

"Why do you insist on only seeing the good?"

Sam pushes his hand through his hair and lets out a slow breath. "I don't know," he says, and the way his words fall, I know he is telling the rock-bottom truth. "I just do."

20

When I go into Ida's on the first Monday of the new year, Greta is back in the shop.

"Sorry about missing work on Saturday," I say to Ida. "You were still out when we came by and then the storm hit. Were you somewhere safe?"

"Oh yes," Ida says, snipping her scissors through a swath of red satin. "I had to stay at the carpenter's shop all night, but it was fine." She finishes her cut and lays the scissors down. "Having another hat block will allow us to work alongside each other. I'll be able to train you. But enough about work, tell me about Nettie. Is there news?"

I am so happy Ida wants to train me on hat forms but that good news is dampened by Nettie's situation. "They've moved her somewhere else and I feel like it's my fault."

"You are a child," Ida says, coming to my side and cradling my hands in hers. "None of this is your fault. Do you remember how I told you our saying, *Liebe ist wie Wasser*— Love is like water?" She looks out the front window of her shop. "And how are things at the boardinghouse? Is it time to move here with me?"

I consider telling her about sleeping in the henhouse and how Miss Franny treated us when Sam talked us back inside, but decide against it. "Quinn really gets along with Sam," I say. "It's important for him to have a friend."

"And your Franny lady is behaving?"

"She's trying," I lie.

"Good," she says in the way she does, which really means *fair* or *satisfactory*. "Perhaps we should eat. Greta, come upstairs with us. I will open my new jar of jam and slice some bread."

Just then the door swings open with a tinkling of bells and Quinn sticks his head in. "Found a newspaper in the street, Ailis. I'll leave it here so it doesn't blow away while I'm playing."

"Thanks," I say as he places a copy of the *Chicago Evening Journal* on a table.

He starts to leave but Ida stops him. "You must eat with us. I'll lock the door for a minute and we will go together."

Quinn takes the paper on his way toward the back stair-well leading up to Ida's apartment.

"Why do you read that garbage?" Ida points to the paper. "They call it news, but it is mostly fable and gossip."

"I know," Quinn says, "but some of it is true."

"Who can tell the difference when it's all reported the same way?" Ida pulls the paper from his hands and tosses it in her garbage basket at the top of the stairs. "That paper seems to publish the worst stories. Bah!"

Quinn and Greta go into her apartment but I am frozen on the top stair, my eyes fixed on the folded *Journal* in the garbage basket.

"Come, *Liebling*," Ida says after the others are inside. "Something sweet will make your heart feel lighter, if even for a moment."

"You're right," I say, still frozen. "They do publish out-landish stories."

"The more outlandish the story, the more papers they sell, I suppose," Ida says.

"And people *do* tend to believe what they read."

"Fools."

I look up at Ida, wide-eyed. "Maybe we should take our story to the newspapers."

Ida raises her hands to her cheeks. "That's it. The news-paper is our answer! We must speak to them today."

Ida asks Greta to mind the shop while she takes us over to the newspaper office. When the *Chicago Tribune* building burned down in the fire, the employees moved into the same building on Canal Street that holds the *Chicago Evening Journal* offices. We decide to stand outside the main entrance and wait until we see a reporter, which only takes about twenty minutes.

"You a reporter?" Quinn asks a young man with a pad of paper in his hand and a couple of pencils jammed into the rim of his derby hat.

"Sure am, kid. Working here for our own *Evening Journal.*"

"Perfect," Quinn says, knowing the *Journal* is far more likely to run our article than the more mainstream *Tribune.* "We've got a story for you."

The man looks Quinn over. "No, thanks." He starts up the stairs.

"It's guaranteed to sell papers," Ida says, stepping up. "I imagine a top story could really help a man's career in this type of business. Of course, if you'd rather we speak to another reporter—maybe one with more experience . . ."

The man eases around on his heel. "What exactly are you saying?"

Ida leans in and says, "The story of the year. Crime, intrigue, helpless children disappearing from right under our noses. Still, if you're not interested . . ."

"Who said I'm not interested?" The reporter slips one of those pencils out of his hatband and begins tapping it on the notepad. "Keep talking."

Ida holds a palm up and looks from side to side. "Not here," she says. "The children are cold and someone might overhear us. Take us to a café. Buy these two a piece of pie. Their memories work better when they are warm and their stomachs are full."

The reporter shoves his pencil back into his hat. "This better be good."

"You won't be sorry," Ida promises.

So we trudge over to a small café where the reporter buys us each a piece of apple pie with clotted cream. Then Quinn and I sit shoulder to shoulder and tell him everything. All about Father Farlane seeing Charlie with the children at church. We tell him how we saw Nettie gathering dead rats in the sewer and how they are staying in the ruins of the Monroe Hotel and at least one other place we don't know about. And how Nettie was taken away as soon as they saw us sniffing around. We follow the advice Ida gave us on the way over to the newspaper office and spare no detail. Quinn even throws in some extra bits about hearing children wailing inside the hotel and begging for water and freedom. It is probably true on some level.

"All these kids are orphans, you say?" I can tell the reporter considers it a problem.

"Oh, no." Ida jumps in. "We've heard some are children being stolen right out of their beds, under the noses of their loving parents. They're beaten and forced into slavery, and for what? A couple of dollars!" Then she reaches over and taps her finger on his notepad. "Now, you tell me the threat of having your child taken from your own hearth, forced to gather diseased rats, and drink only sewer water won't sell a stack of newspapers."

Quinn looks at me. We both know it is likely orphan children who fill the hotel, but we also know that fact is a lot less newsworthy. "Maybe you could headline the article *Will Your Child Be Next?*" Quinn suggests.

Ida claps her hands together. "That's a powerful headline, Quinn. Well done!"

"Excuse me," the reporter says. "I'll be the one writing the headline. If I decide to write anything at all." He tucks his pencil back, slides his notepad into his coat, and stands up. "I hope you enjoyed the pie."

"Yes, sir," I say, running my finger along my bottom lip, checking for remnants of cream. "You'll write the article, won't you?"

"It's not so easy. Absolute Exterminators is an important business for Chicago and Mr. Blume is a man of significant influence."

"Think of the children," Ida pleads. "The helpless, innocent souls. And here you are, the only brave knight able to help them. A story like this can make a career."

"You mean obliterate it," the man mumbles.

Ida grabs his sleeve. "A brave knight. That is what the families of our city need. It's what the readers of the newspaper need. You are our one hope."

He leaves us sitting at a corner table in the café, clotted cream turning sour in our stomachs.

"Do you think he'll write the article?" I ask.

Ida twists her napkin in her hands and looks out the frost-laden window to some far-off place. "Only heaven knows."

21

It is a fragile line between heartbreak and fury, and I teeter between the two over the next few days. Each morning Quinn and I rush to finish our chores and be freed from Miss Franny's grasp. Then we pick up a copy of the *Journal* on our way to work, hoping to find our story about Chicago's hidden rat slaves, but it's never there. I get so angry at the printing of meaningless stories about city hall's new funding or announcements regarding the Ladies' Aid Society meetings. We even try talking to another reporter—an older gentleman—who walks away from us mid-sentence the moment we mention Mr. Blume's name.

Cowards, the lot of them.

When Saturday comes, I find myself out on the shore of

Lake Michigan watching the sunrise. Patches of thick fog hover above the icy, black water. The sun pushes up out of the earth on the far shore. The frozen lake shimmers and radiates with the golden reflection of an emerging day and, despite the freezing temperature, I am glad to be there.

"Where'd you go?" Quinn asks when I return to Miss Franny's. He is barely awake.

"To the outhouse," I say, wanting to keep the lake to myself.

He wraps his blanket around his shoulders. "Ailis?" he asks, and I know to sit down on the side of the bed. "Do you ever think we'll go back home?"

"To Peshtigo? What's there for us?"

Quinn pulls his knees up and rests his chin on them, and I remember he is only eleven—a boy. And I only a girl, really. "They're still there. At least their grave is."

We only dug one grave. Quinn fashioned one large coffin from singed scraps of wood and buried them together. "But the town is completely destroyed. At least here there's a good part of the city left. Shops and schools and churches. You've heard about Mayor Medill's speeches. Chicago will rise up and become greater than ever before."

I am trying to humor him with my impression but he holds his solemn expression and says, "I dreamed of them again last night. Father just came in from skimming cranberries. His shirt was wet and his hair was matted down the way it gets from his hat. Mother was stirring a pot over the fire and singing 'Katie-Ba-Loo' to Gertrude." He squints. "I can't remember what Gertrude was doing, but she was there, too."

I think of Mother and sing a refrain from the song:

Katie-Ba-Loo, the mountain sings
Its song of wondrous love.
Oh, Katie-Ba-Loo, go to your home
Fly quickly as the dove.

Quinn joins me for the chorus:

Katie-Ba-Loo, Katie-Ba-Ree,
please give your heart to me.

It's a soft, lilting tune and we fade off on the last words of the chorus, leaving the room silent.

"Do you want to go back?" I ask.

"Maybe someday."

"I think it would make me sad to see our old farm."

Quinn looks down and nods.

"And we both agreed we're tired of being sad. What about our promise to only remember the good times?"

"My dream was about the good times."

"True," I say, realizing good times don't always have to bring laughter. There's the quiet kind of happiness, too. "And that song is beautiful."

"I should learn how to play it on the fiddle."

"Definitely," I say. "But first we have work to do."

"Will you go to Ida's this morning?" Quinn asks.

"She's expecting me in a couple of hours."

Quinn walks over to the little window and says, "At least the sun is shining. That'll make for more people on the streets. It should be a nice day for playing music."

I go out into the kitchen. Singing "Katie-Ba-Loo" with Quinn has made me miss working alongside Mother and so I decide to start breakfast. I promised Sam that I would try harder at getting along with Miss Franny. Maybe serving her in this way will help things between us, even a little.

First, I get fresh water and begin boiling it for morning coffee. Next, I fill the wooden bowl with wheat kernels, crush them into flour with the pestle, and mix in baking soda, salt, oil, and two eggs. I pull out a cast-iron skillet, line it with oil, and warm it on the stove. After a few minutes, I dip my fingers into the bucket and drop a few beads of water into the skillet. They crackle and bounce and that's how I know it is hot enough to start the pancakes.

"I'll take two fresh ones off the top," Miss Franny says,

coming into the kitchen and looking over my shoulder. "Don't make the coffee too strong. Watering it down makes it last longer." I'm surprised she doesn't mention anything about me making breakfast. Instead, she drops into a chair at the dining room table and waits for me to serve her. All the while I'm flipping pancakes, pulling out jam, and making coffee. "And don't make the pancakes too big, either," she says from her seat. "We don't need to be giving away the farm."

I serve her two perfect pancakes with jam and butter and hot coffee—watered down appropriately. After she eats, she comes over and takes the serving platter of pancakes to give to the guests. "Dishes," is all she says to me, which I pretend to mean, *Delicious pancakes, Ailis. How kind of you to make them for me. Would you mind doing the dishes whilst I serve these pancakes to the guests coming downstairs and claim full credit for them?* I must be smiling because she stops in her tracks and says, "What?"

"Nothing, Miss Franny."

"Then get to it."

"Yes, ma'am."

The next hour is washing dishes, sweeping floors, wiping the table, and helping Quinn sprinkle sand on the frozen front walkway so it's less slippery.

Sam has picked up extra hours at the iron smith so he walks with us for a block and a half on our way into the city.

"Play your heart out," he says to Quinn when we get to Van Buren Street and he goes his own way.

"Always do," Quinn says. Then he turns to me. "Let's grab a newspaper."

"I don't want to be late," I say, tired of looking for our story.

"Suit yourself, but I'm going to find one." He peels off a block before Ida's.

"Where will you be playing today?" I holler after him.

"Don't worry, I'll find a fire pit close by." He turns around, walking backward, and raises his fiddle case high in the air. "Just follow the music."

• • •

I notice a black-and-white kitten sitting at Ida's feet when I walk into the shop. Ida is at her table, cutting squares of burgundy satin. Her scissor blades glint silver against the mottled sunlight streaming in the front window.

"Good morning, *Liebling*," she says in an especially cheerful tone.

"Good morning," I say.

The kitten tries to jump up against Ida's chair leg but topples over onto the tip of her shoe. "Aye, *Katze*," she says, putting her scissors aside and reaching down. "If you are to live in this shop, you must learn to stay out of the way."

"He's darling," I say.

"He is feisty," she says. "And wonderful. Greta gave him to me."

Greta comes in from the storeroom just then and says, "Our cat at home had kittens and my father sent one as a thank-you for the work Ida has given me. He will grow to be a good mouser." She places a basket on the floor. "Here is what I could find in the storeroom."

"That will work." Ida hands her the cat.

Greta folds a piece of scrap fabric into the bottom of the basket and places the kitten inside.

"Where would you like me to start today?" I ask.

Ida stands up. "My back is aching and it's still so early in the day. Maybe you can take over and let me stand for a moment."

I've cut trim, processed orders, and organized incoming stock but Ida has always been the one to make the actual pattern pieces for the hats. "Really?" I ask, feeling a rush of excitement.

"Because of my back," she says, but the way her eyes gleam lets me know she understands the meaning of her offer.

I sit down in her chair. She smells like a blend of coffee

and mint, leaning over my shoulder and lining two paper squares along the edge of the table. "I need eight more of these," she says as she points to the first pattern piece, "and four more of these," as she points to the second. "Be sure to cut carefully around the corners."

Her scissors—the ones that she always uses—feel cool and heavy in my hand. I can't help but glance over at Greta, who is smiling at me.

"I will," I say.

At that moment, Quinn rushes in the front door. He is flapping a newspaper up over his head and nearly out of breath. "It's here," he shouts as if we were a mile away. "The article is here!" He stops, sets his fiddle down, and leans over, resting his hands on his knees and catching his breath.

"Can it be true?" Ida asks.

"I heard the newsie hollering out the headline," Quinn says. "He was saying, '*Will Your Child Be Next? Chicago's Children Forced into the Rat Trade.*'"

"That's your headline!" I say, coming out from around the table.

"I know!" He shoves the paper into my chest.

I sit down right there on the floor of Ida's shop and begin reading out loud. "*Will Your Child Be Next? Chicago's Children Forced into the Rat Trade, by Anonymous.* So *that's* how he avoided getting in trouble."

"Read it!" Ida and Quinn say at the same time from above me.

"*Trusted sources inform the* Journal *that Chicago's own children are being plucked off the streets and tossed into a veritable den of iniquity in the underground rat trade.*" I look up. "That's good writing."

Quinn makes a hand motion that means, *Go on.*

"It tells everything! The location of the hotel and how the children are being starved of water and food. It even says *Absolute Exterminators*, right here!" I point to the words and Quinn leans in, mouthing them as if he can fully read.

And then, just like Quinn the moment before, Sam comes bursting through the front door. It's odd to see him standing among the lace and delicate wares.

"Did you hear?" he asks.

"We just got the news," Quinn says.

Sam steps forward and nods to Ida. "Ma'am."

"Sam is our friend from the boardinghouse," Quinn explains.

"Word has it the police are headed over to the Monroe to investigate," Sam says. "Let's go."

Ida notices that I look over to her scissors and she says, "We will continue the lesson later."

"What about the shop?" I ask.

Greta steps forward. "I'll stay behind with the kitten."

"No," Ida says. "We will all go. This is important and our little *Katze* must manage himself."

We leave a small bowl of water for the kitten and lock up the shop. As we near Monroe Street we hear chanting rising up into the icy blue sky. "Down with Absolute! Down with Absolute! Down with Absolute!"

"How many people are there?" Quinn asks, taking off in a sprint.

We round the corner and are stopped by throngs of people outside of the hotel.

"Look at it!" Ida exclaims. "All from your good idea to talk to the newspaper!"

I can hardly see the hotel for the crowd.

And the noise! Everyone is jabbing their fists into the air and chanting in unison, "Down with Absolute!"

Within seconds, the police arrive. There are at least two dozen officers in full uniforms with wooden batons and guns hanging from their belts. My heart soars at the sight of the crowd parting and the officers marching up to the hotel.

A hush falls as one officer steps forward and bangs on the door.

Silence.

He pulls out his club and slams it against the door. "Open in the name of the law!" He looks to his mates and then stands back, raises a foot, and kicks the door down.

The crowd goes wild, shoving forward and shouting things like, *Free the children!* And, *Don't let Mr. Blume escape!* And, *Catch the rat!* Ida grabs my hand, I take Greta's hand, and we try to stay close behind Sam and Quinn as the crowd pushes forward.

"Stay together!" Sam yells above the shouting.

It's mayhem and I think I'm about to be crushed alive when, at once, everyone starts to back up, making room for the police officers who are shoving a row of men out the front of the hotel. As they are led to the police wagons, I notice an officer purposely shoves one of the thugs extra hard, causing him to fall down on the dirt road, then lifts him up by the collar and pushes him forward again.

"Gracious," Ida says as the children slowly start coming out. They squint their eyes against the morning light and seem unsure of the freedom being offered up.

A few women—probably from the Ladies' Aid Society— rush forward to help lead the children over to the side of the yard where two more police officers are pulling out their notebooks and asking questions.

"Too bad Net's not in there," Sam says.

It's miserable to know she could have been freed today if Quinn and I hadn't caused her to be moved to a different location.

"But surely this is not the end," Ida says. "Now they will be able to search for other hideouts, yes?"

"Let's hope so," Quinn says, but regret has spoiled hope for me.

Sam guesses my thoughts and says, "What you guys did is something else. You helped a lot of kids today."

Then he gives a quick pat to Quinn's shoulder. "It looks like things are taken care of here. We'll see you tonight?"

"Sure," Quinn says.

Sam saunters down the road. I find a pile of charred bricks and sit down. "Now what?"

Greta joins me and wraps her arms around her knees.

"Look," Ida says, and I notice a splendid carriage down the street, on the opposite side of the hotel. "I've seen that in the city before. I believe it belongs to Mr. Olsen. Perhaps he has returned."

I stand and look. It is very fine.

And stepping out the door is someone painfully small and frail.

I put my hand on my heart and suck in my breath. "Nettie."

Nettie nearly snaps in two for all the hugs we are giving her. Quinn even spins around in a circle when he hugs her, sending her bony legs out in a flutter.

"How'd you find her?" I ask Mr. Olsen.

"When I received your message and read this morning's edition of the *Journal*, I knew it would be best to pay a visit to Mr. Blume."

"What did he say?" Quinn asks.

"Naturally he denied any involvement, but I was eventually able to convince him to track the girl down at another building across town and sell her back to me."

"You bought her?"

"I negotiated her freedom."

"Is that legal?" I ask.

Mr. Olsen looks across the street to the Monroe. The police wagons have carted off the adults but the children are still being questioned. "I felt it important to circumvent the legal process and find the girl as soon as possible."

I keep hold of Nettie's hand, patting it gently. "Thank you," I say to him. "I'm sure we can never repay you."

Mr. Olsen looks down at me. "You are not without resources, Ailis Doyle."

"What resources do I have?" I ask, confused.

"We shall speak of that later. Our charge at the moment is the child. Quick, all of you, into the carriage. Let us return to my home for a feast befitting this momentous occasion."

Quinn leans in. "Does that mean lunch?"

"I think so," I whisper back.

All six of us pile into Mr. Olsen's carriage. Nettie sits on my lap. She is so light, I wouldn't have felt her if it weren't for the bones of her bottom poking into my legs. How little she must have eaten, I think, to lose so much weight in only twenty-four days. I wrap my arms around her waist and pull her in close, careful not to squeeze too hard. "I'm so glad you're back."

"Only for today, right?"

"No, Nettie," I say. "Forever."

"But what about the rats?"

"Who cares about the stupid rats?"

Ida touches my knee. "Now, child," she says to Nettie. "Forgive Ailis. She doesn't understand how important your work was."

What is she talking about?

Ida keeps on. "But you must understand the work you were doing should be performed by adults. It is their worry, not yours. Their job, not a child's."

"Big people can't fit into some of the tunnels," she says. "They need me."

"You are very important, it's true," Ida says in a soothing tone, easing her words out and maintaining a warm smile. "Still, the police commissioner has decided children should go to school and be with their families, so that is what we shall do."

"I don't have a family," Nettie says.

"You have us," I say.

Nettie leans back into me and points to Ida and Greta. "I don't know who these people are."

Ida gives a gentle laugh and introduces herself, along with Greta. "We are a hodgepodge of people, but we love you very much. Isn't that what makes a family after all?"

Nettie is chewing on her bottom lip and rubbing her hand under her nose. "I guess so."

"Then it is settled," Ida says.

Nettie turns to Mr. Olsen. "Are you part of the family, too?"

I start to apologize, but Mr. Olsen raises his hand. "As much as I can be, yes."

That makes Nettie smile so wide her cheeks force her puffy eyes closed. "Since you're part of the family, can I ask you a question?"

"Of course."

"Can I keep my chicken, Kristina, at your house?"

Mr. Olsen laughs. "I will see to it myself."

• • •

We start in Mr. Olsen's kitchen, which is the size of seven or eight normal kitchens. He cuts an apple for Nettie and requests that his maid make slices of honeyed bread and glasses of warm milk for us all.

"To tide you over," he says. "A proper meal will take time to prepare."

Fresh honeyed bread and a tall glass of warm milk is more than any meal I am used to so I can't begin to imagine what will come next.

A chestnut-skinned woman bustles into the kitchen with her arms full of towels and stops in her tracks. "Is this the girl?" She is looking at Nettie.

"It is," Mr. Olsen says. "And we're planning a feast to celebrate her freedom."

The woman looks Nettie over and asks, "Is there time for a bath?"

"Oh, yes," Mr. Olsen says. "She's all yours, Carlene."

The woman sets the towels on the counter and goes to Nettie, mumbling about how she needs a decent bath and someone to look at her cuts and bruises. "And we'll get ointment for those eyes. I'll send for Dr. Brown immediately." She scoops Nettie into her arms and takes her out of the room.

"Carlene will use great care tending to the girl," Mr. Olsen assures me.

It's not that I don't trust Carlene. I'm just not ready to have Nettie leave me, even if it is only to another part of the house.

Ida takes my hand. "She will be fine." Her fingers are soft around mine.

"You are welcome to wait for her, and for our meal, in the library," Mr. Olsen says. "If you will excuse me, there are a few items requiring my attention."

"What about paying you back?" I ask, remembering what he said.

Mr. Olsen turns at the door. "Business always follows the meal. It's the way of the world." He disappears down the hallway.

Quinn doesn't have to be asked twice to go to the library and we follow the maid's directions down the hall, turning right at the golden elephant statue.

"Quite a library," Ida says.

"Amazing," Greta agrees.

Quinn runs his fingers up and down the spines of the books, like he is imagining what adventure each holds.

"Do you have a favorite?" Greta asks at his side.

I know Quinn wishes he were a better reader and am afraid for him to answer so I say, "He likes Irish authors and Irish fables."

He shoots me a look and I clamp my lips together.

"I was needed in our cranberry bogs," he says, and she smiles, understanding.

I sink down into a worn leather chair and tuck my knees under me like a cat curling into a cushion. I must have dozed off because I am startled awake by a bell and the butler standing at the library door announcing our meal.

We follow Mr. Olsen's butler into the dining room. My wildest dreams couldn't match what is laid before us on the table. A haunch of venison, a tureen of clam soup, baked potatoes in jackets, turnips with onion sauce, pickled cabbage, crabapple jelly with butter-flake rolls, and a leaf-shaped glass dish with sweet pickled grapes. But what catches Nettie's attention is the embroidered linen cloth underneath it all.

"It's so pretty," she says, holding the corner up and show-ing us green leaves stitched into a circle pattern.

"*You're* so pretty," Ida says back.

Ida is right. While I slept, Nettie was transformed from a street urchin into something out of a picture book. Her skin is pink and clean, her hair is combed and parted, with a white tulle bow, and she is wearing a navy dress with a train stitched across the chest. Even her eyes look better.

"Luckily, the neighbor girl is almost this same size," Carlene says, motioning to Nettie's dress. "Also, Dr. Brown has prescribed this ointment for the girl's eyes." She hands a vial to Ida. "It should be administered morning and night."

It makes sense for her to give the medicine to Ida because she is the adult in our group of visitors. But it makes me wonder where we will all go from here. Back to Miss Franny's? In with Ida? Watching Nettie gawk and gaze around the house, I can guess she is imagining herself here with Mr. Olsen, but I know that won't happen. When Nettie asked him if he'd be part of our family group, his answer was qualified. *As much as I can be,* he said. Which isn't exactly the same as *Move in with me tomorrow.*

When Mr. Olsen comes into the room, we take our seats and begin our meal. It is difficult not to scoop everything onto my plate but I manage to *show restraint* as Miss Franny would say and take only a small portion of each item.

Mr. Olsen speaks of his discussion with the police department and how he is certain they will investigate other locations where Absolute Exterminators kept children.

"Where will the children go?" Quinn asks.

"An excellent question, my boy," Mr. Olsen says. "I have spoken with Mayor Medill myself and he assures me they will find suitable accommodations for each child."

"What about Charlie?" I ask, speaking through a mouthful of turnips.

"Apprehended," Mr. Olsen says.

I look over to Nettie, whose fork is frozen in front of her mouth with a piece of venison dangling from the tines. She lowers it back to her plate and says, "Is Charlie in trouble?"

We all look to Ida, who seems to be the only one who knows how to talk to Nettie.

"No, child," she says. "He has been given another job is all."

We plaster on smiles and nod in agreement. It is probably best not to upset Nettie any further.

I go back to my turnips and pickled grapes, which are tangy and sweet at the same time. Mr. Olsen changes the subject and speaks of his travels, asking Ida all about Germany. Quinn and Greta make eyes at each other and I almost remind him he is only eleven years old and she about the same age, but decide to let it go. Father and Mother first met at a town dance when they were only eleven.

I suppose love has to start somewhere.

Nettie eats a small portion of the food on her plate and then slumps down in her chair and falls asleep. Carlene comes and carries her off to a soft spot.

"Ailis," Mr. Olsen says once we are at the end of our meal. "May I speak with you in my office?"

I fold the cloth napkin from my lap, place it next to my plate, and say, "Of course."

He turns to Ida. "I would appreciate her having an adult confidante for this discussion. Would you join us?"

Ida agrees and follows us into Mr. Olsen's office, which is dark mahogany, emerald rugs, and yellow glass lamplight in every direction. I think of the contrast of this space to the worn pine table Father did his paperwork on.

"Please sit," Mr. Olsen says, directing us to two chairs across from where he is taking a seat behind his desk. "Ailis," he begins, "as you know, I thought highly of your father. He was a liaison between the railroad and the people of Peshtigo—a friend in business and, in my mind, a friend in life."

"Father spoke highly of you as well," I say.

"What you may not know is, I have long wanted to build a line from Chicago up through Wisconsin. Your farm in Peshtigo sits at the base of where we need to build. The reason I approached your father was because the railroad wanted to buy his land—to allow access, you see."

"I remember Father saying something about that, but he would never sell our land."

"At the time, no, he wouldn't. And I understood his position, even if that meant we were unable to move forward with the building of that rail line. But now circumstances have changed."

"You've seen it yourself," I say. "The town is gone."

"Make no mistake, Peshtigo will rebuild," he says. "Perhaps not as quickly as Chicago, but there are enough people who will stay. Having the railroad go through will assure they can rebuild faster."

"You still want to buy our farm?"

"As a previous president of the Union Pacific Railroad, I guarantee you a fair price."

I lean back in my chair, thinking.

Mr. Olsen takes my silence as uncertainty and says, "Selling your land will help dozens, maybe even hundreds of others rebuild. And it goes without saying you and your brother will have free access to that rail line. Anytime you wish to visit Peshtigo and your family's grave site, you are guaranteed a first-class seat."

"First class," Ida breathes.

"What will become of us?" I ask, knowing Mr. Olsen isn't the one who can answer that question.

He opens a drawer in his desk, pulls out a booklet, and scribbles something down. "I intended to have this discussion shortly after the fires, but urgent business took my attention for a time. I am sincerely sorry it has taken me this long. Here is my offer." He hands me a promissory note. "The Union Pacific's new line would ideally run right through your property. We could build around it, of course, but your farm has always been a key component of our plan."

Ida leans in and whispers, "Properly used, that will set you up for a lifetime."

I press the note down into my lap and hear Ida whispering to me on my left side, but I also feel something else. Someone on my right side saying, *Now is the time. Don't be afraid to tell them what you need, Ailis.*

I turn to my right but there is no one there. Still, the words remain.

"I want to move into a larger apartment with you, Ida. Quinn and Nettie, too." I imagine the look on Nettie's face when she sees Ida's new kitten. She will be smitten.

A grin spreads out on Ida's face. "There is a three-room apartment vacant just two floors above mine. I am tired of my dingy old place anyway. You will be doing me a favor taking me away from that miserable box."

"I want to be your apprentice and I want Nettie to get her education." I look back at the promissory note. "Will this be enough for her college?"

"I will ensure the girl's college. It would be my pleasure," Mr. Olsen offers. "But I insist you finish school yourself, Ailis. It is what your father would have wanted."

I close my eyes and imagine Father standing right next to my chair with his strong, weathered hand on my shoulder, saying those words again: *Don't be afraid to tell them*. I reach into my skirt pocket and pull out the card from the music school. It is warped from being carried around and from being in the wet gutter, but you can still read the words:

GRAND SCHOOL OF MUSIC
Chicago, Illinois
Robert Donlope, Director

"Okay," I say. "If I can apprentice under Ida after my classes." Then I add, "And I want Quinn to go to this school. A three-room apartment, college for Nettie someday, and this music school for Quinn. If I can have those things, I will sell you Father's land."

"Your land," Mr. Olsen says.

I touch the promissory note. "And Quinn's. I should ask him about this."

Mr. Olsen agrees. "Of course. I'll wait here."

I walk down the hallway into the library where Greta is

sitting next to Quinn on the couch, reading aloud from a book.

"Can I have a moment?" I ask.

She closes the book and steps out.

"Is everything okay?" Quinn asks.

"Mr. Olsen wants to buy our farm in Peshtigo for the railroad. If we agree, we will be able to move into a larger apartment with Ida. Nettie can stay with us, too." I hold out Mr. Donlope's calling card. "And we could pay for you to go to this music school."

"I told you, I'm too old to start school."

"You're too young to walk away from something this important," I say.

Quinn takes the card and tries to straighten it out, pressing the bent corner between his finger and thumb. "I threw this in the gutter," he says.

"And I took it out. Look, Quinn, I know you're nervous, but I also know you have a gift. If you can't do this for yourself, do it for Father's memory. Do it so we can have the future they would have wanted for us."

"I don't know about living with Ida," he says. "Does she really want us there? What about Sam?"

"She really does. And Sam will always be your friend," I say. "But it's time for us to find our own way. And give Nettie the family she deserves."

He keeps his head down but gradually, slowly nods. "Okay," he says.

I go back into Mr. Olsen's office. He is deep in discussion with Ida and, when he sees me, says, "It is becoming clear there are issues with the management of my boardinghouse. I am sorry to have been so unaware."

I glance at Ida, who raises a shoulder in confession. I don't want her to feel bad so I sit next to her and say, "Miss Franny's not the best with children." As soon as the words come, I think, *not the best with children*? Here is my golden opportunity to rightfully fillet Miss Franny and serve her up on a platter to her employer, but all I can manage is *not the best*?

"I see," Mr. Olsen says. "She's been with me for many years and I know she came from difficult circumstances, but maybe I can find another place for her within my organization."

"That might be a good idea."

Mr. Olsen seems satisfied. "Now that we've settled that matter, what is your brother's opinion of my offer?"

"Oh, yes," I say, leaning across his desk and reaching my hand out. "We have a deal."

"Wonderful!"

As his warm palm presses against mine, I think of the grubby cinnamon moon on the night we lost everything and how it turned back to its clean white color so easily.

And the thought comes to me that life inches forward moment by moment, day by day. That today will end—whether we are ready for it to end or not—and that a new tomorrow will always come. And I suppose the only choice we ever *really* have is to allow ourselves to splinter against the weight of it all or to dig down, gather courage, and walk on.

AUTHOR'S NOTE

The idea for this novel came to me when I read about a violin that survived the horrendous Peshtigo, Wisconsin, fire of 1871 because its owner buried it deep in the ground. The thought of that violin and the curiosity of who owned it stayed with me. Shortly after reading that story, I visited Chicago and heard the most beautiful violin music being played by an immigrant under a bridge by Lake Michigan. These elements merged to become the Doyle family's fiddle and story. Additionally, I have long been intrigued by the tragic plight of Catherine O'Leary.

My personal family history is a blend of Irish, French, and German immigrants and I pulled from that for this novel. The character Ida Muench was inspired by my great-grandmother's sister, Ida Dixon, who ran a millinery shop in the early 1900s and never had any children of her own. I imagine she would have taken in Ailis, Quinn, and Nettie had they crossed her path.

FIRESTORM: PESHTIGO, WISCONSIN

The deadliest fire in American history took place in Peshtigo, Wisconsin, on Sunday, October 8, 1871. Like the Great Chicago Fire, which occurred on the same day, the origins of the Peshtigo fire remain a mystery. Thousands of acres were destroyed in and around Peshtigo and an estimated 2,400 lives were lost, although records were sparse and bodies were burned beyond recognition, making a true count difficult. What differentiates Peshtigo's fire from most others is that it was reported to be a rare phenomenon: a fire fueled by a tornado. Survivors recorded finding glass spun along the roots of felled trees, indicating temperatures inside the fire-tornado that must have reached in excess of 3,200 degrees Fahrenheit. Compare that number to the typical 450–800 degrees of a regular forest fire and it is easy to understand the depth of devastation that took place in Peshtigo on that fateful day.

Like fictional Ailis and Quinn, a small number of residents survived the fire by jumping into the Menominee River. Also like the characters in this novel, many of the survivors left Peshtigo, hoping to find a new life in other cities. Peshtigo, Wisconsin, still exists today and there is a small monument erected in memory of those who lost their lives in the 1871 firestorm.

THE GREAT CHICAGO FIRE

The Great Chicago Fire also occurred on Sunday, October 8, 1871, taking approximately 250 to 300 lives. It did, indeed, begin in the barn of Patrick and Catherine O'Leary, who were exonerated of all charges in the months after the fire. The cause of the Chicago fire remains unknown.

Joseph Medill was publisher of the *Chicago Tribune* at the time and ran for the office of mayor on the "Fireproof Ticket" in November, winning by a landslide. He was instrumental in reaching out to other states and nations, soliciting donations, and spearheading the rebuilding effort that would forever change the destiny of Chicago and make it one of the greatest cities of its time. Chicago was in a state of turmoil and disorder in the weeks following the fire. Much of the city was a dangerous and desolate place. Still, tourists poured in from around the country, hoping to get a glimpse of the devastation.

MRS. O'LEARY AND THE NEWSPAPERS

One of the heartbreaking results of the Great Chicago Fire was the story of Catherine O'Leary. While the fire did start in her barn, she steadfastly maintained her innocence, stating that she and her family were asleep at the time the fire began. For some unknown reason, a reporter from the *Chicago Evening Journal* (which later became the *Chicago Times*) decided to write a fraudulent article wherein he described that Mrs. O'Leary was: "Apparently about 70 years of age, and was bent almost double with the weight of many years of toil, and trouble, and privation. Her dress corresponded with her demands, being ragged and dirty in the extreme." In truth, Catherine O'Leary was only in her forties at the time of the fire and denied ever speaking to the newspaper reporter. He further stated in his article that she admitted to setting the fire intentionally when city officials denied her welfare claim, writing: "The old hag swore she would be revenged on a city that would deny her a bit of wool or a pound of bacon." Catherine O'Leary ran a successful milk business and was never the recipient of state assistance. In her statement to the investigative council, she asked the poignant question of why, if she was accused of seeking revenge on the city, she would set the fire in her *own* barn, causing her to lose her business and threatening the lives of her own family members.

Later, this reporter admitted to making up the story in an effort to sell newspapers, but few people paid attention to the article's retraction. The damage was done and Catherine O'Leary spent her remaining years avoiding public interaction.

The newspaper articles from the *Chicago Evening Journal* and the *Chicago Tribune* mentioned in the novel are historically correct as they pertain to Mrs. O'Leary and the Fire Commission's investigation. The portion about Absolute Exterminators is fiction.

MR. OLSEN

The character of Mr. Olsen in this novel is loosely based on Mr. William Butler Ogden. William Butler Ogden was elected Chicago's first mayor in 1837. He held properties in Peshtigo, Chicago, and New York, and was a man of great influence with many political connections. He was also elected the first president of the Union Pacific Railroad in 1862 and worked tirelessly to extend the railroad from Chicago through Michigan and eventually out West.

WHAT HAPPENED TO NETTIE

Child labor has been a part of societies throughout all human history. It was at an all-time high during the years following the Great Chicago Fire due to the Industrial Revolution. Children were considered useful because their small size allowed them to access areas of machinery or work where adults could not fit. They were also considered more expendable and less expensive than their adult counterparts. By the year 1900, as many as two million children under the age of sixteen were employed in the United States, with half of those children under the age of twelve. Homeless children were at the mercy of strangers and it was not uncommon for them to be preyed upon and sold into various trades such as chimney sweeping, mining, textile mill work, and even rat catching. Tragically, child exploitation still exists today. Though less overt, and now illegal in the United States, it is not unheard of. To learn more, visit the National Center for Missing and Exploited Children at missingkids.org.

SELECTED BIBLIOGRAPHY

BOOKS AND PERIODICALS

Bales, Richard F. "Did the Cow Do It?: A New Look at the Cause of the Great Chicago Fire." *Journal of the Illinois State Historical Society,* vol. 90 (1997).

————. *The Great Chicago Fire and the Myth of Mrs. O'Leary's Cow.* Jefferson, NC: McFarland and Company, Inc., 2002.

Gess, Denise, and William Lutz. *Firestorm at Peshtigo: A Town, Its People, and the Deadliest Fire in American History.* New York: Henry Holt and Company, 2002.

Knickelbine, Scott. *The Great Peshtigo Fire: Stories and Science from America's Deadliest Firestorm.* Madison, WI: Wisconsin Historical Society Press, 2012.

Lowe, David Garrard, ed. *The Great Chicago Fire: In Eyewitness Accounts and 70 Contemporary Photographs and Illustrations.* Mineola, NY: Dover Publications, Inc., 1979.

Murphy, Jim. *The Great Fire.* New York: Scholastic Inc., 1995.

Pernin, Peter. *The Great Peshtigo Fire: An Eyewitness Account.* 2nd ed. Madison, WI: Wisconsin Historical Society Press, 1999.

Sawislak, Karen. *Smoldering City: Chicagoans and the Great Fire, 1871–1847.* Chicago: University of Chicago Press, 1995.

DOCUMENTS REVIEWED AND REFERENCED

Chicago Evening Journal, October 9, 1871.

Chicago Evening Journal, October 18, 1871.

Chicago Tribune, November 25, 1871.

Union Fireproof Ticket 11th Ward.

Mayor Roswell B. Mason's handwritten note to release prisoners post-fire, dated October 9, 1871.

Handwritten statement of events from Catherine O'Leary's testimony before the Chicago Fire Commission Investigative Council.

Death certificate for Catherine O'Leary, showing her age at the time of the fire to be forty-four years old.

WEBSITE

greatchicagofire.org